CROW

KIM SHAW

© Kim Shaw 2024

First edition

The right of Kim Shaw to be identified as the author of this work has been asserted to her in accordance with the Copyright, Designs and Patents Act 1988.
    All rights reserved. This book is sold subject to the condition that it shall not, by way of trade or otherwise, be lent, resold, hired out, or otherwise circulated without the publisher's prior consent in any form of binding or cover other than that in which it is published and without a similar condition, including this condition, being imposed on the subsequent purchaser.

ISBN: 978-1-0683664-0-6 (Paperback)
ISBN: 978-1-0683664-1-3 (eBook)

Cover art www.publishingbuddy.co.uk

One

The day Ray's Pa died it didn't rain. It never rained – not in that summer – and that, right there, was the start of it.

Ray lived with Ma and Pa on a run-down homestead out West on a small parcel of government land. The sort that was given to settlers willing to scratch out a living from the hot, dry, cussed earth. It was a landscape that defined their existence - heavy, brown and unrelenting. The dust and dirt coated their world in a dull brown grime, a dismal reflection of their minimal lives. The land itself was harsh, and it made those who lived on it harsh, but strong. Stiff, unmalleable people who fought against the seasons. Living in spite of their surroundings.

Way before she was born, Pa had built the cabin and the barn with the help of the other folk around the town. They helped him like he'd helped them to build their cabins and barns. He planted corn, oats and beets deep in the dry dirt. He hired a plough and horses once a year to turn up the hard baked earth before laying the seeds in long ridged rows. He hauled lumber, chopped wood and hunted meat for the pot. All the time spitting and staring at the sky, cussing the heat, breathing the dust, and crying for rain.

Pa sure was a rough man. Although Ray had lived with him and Ma in the same small cabin her whole life, she wasn't sure she knew him at all. They'd danced around each other, taking up their own space, eyes no more than glancing off each other. His life was toil and predictability. He followed the cycle of day and night, moving seamlessly from the land to the whiskey bottle.

When he wasn't working the land, he was drunk; sometimes a little, usually a lot. At night, she heard him coughing, cussing and swearing, and sometimes fucking her Ma. When he was out, the air changed. It was lighter and clearer, and the silence felt soft. Her Pa wasn't a mean man, nor a hateful one, but he didn't make their lives easy. One thing Ray knew though, life sure got harder after he died.

Ray sensed something bad was going to happen. Sometimes the future seemed to be clear laid out in front of her. She didn't know how, nor even exactly what, some kind of feeling in her belly that good, or bad, was on its way. Pa's drinking had gotten worse. There was more cussing and swearing, and Ma looked like she was wound up so tight, she might just break in two. Ray did her chores in silence, like usual. She helped Ma look after her herb garden. She fetched water from the well, chopped wood for the fire and looked after the horses. That was her best time. She loved those two horses, especially Rio, the small bay. She'd looked after him since they'd got him as a foal. She would rest her forehead on his neck, close her eyes and breathe in his scent. He smelt sweet, like sunshine and freedom. She felt like she could sink in under his skin to become part of him, their heartbeats merging. When she rode, she would sometimes let go of the reins and urge him into a gallop. She felt as if they were one, flying together on the wind. She'd look up at the birds high in the sky performing their aerial dance. C*aaaw caaaw* singing their joy of flight. In those moments, she felt part of Rio, part of nature: she felt free. But in the weeks before Pa died, a feeling of unease swirled around her, no matter what she was doing. It clouded everything, leaving a dull sheen on life.

On that day, Ray rose at sunrise and spent her time as usual busy with chores. As she moved around the homestead the air tasted stale in her mouth. Although there wasn't a cloud in the sky, it was dull, as if the sun itself was coated by a layer of dust. After seeing to the horses, she stood outside the barn. A single raven was perfecting its mournful dance in the hazy sky. Its sweeping and swirling hypnotic pattern made her sway in time to its movements. It distracted her from the feeling of anxiety that sat in the pit of her stomach.

By the time the sun had slid past midday, Pa had already started on the whiskey bottle. By the time he'd finished the day's work, he was drunk. He was so addled, he couldn't even mount his horse, not without a block to stand on. Without a word or a wave, he rode off toward the town, cocked sideways on his saddle. A half empty bottle hung from his hand. In minutes, he was swallowed by the wave of dust kicked up by the hooves. The sun was low in the sky, but Ray could still feel its unrelenting heat. She watched the billow of dust until it disappeared beneath the horizon.

Later that night, after it got dark, Ma sat by the fire pounding out dried herbs. Ray sat on a stool beside her, melting candle stubs and casting sideways glances at her. She looked like a shadow woman, pale and grey, her eyes so deep in her head they were hard to see. Her breathing was rough and every few minutes she coughed; her shoulders heaved, and her eyes watered with the effort.

'Ma, are you feeling well'?

'I'm just tired girl, like always, but I'll be fine. Just got to get me these herbs ground is all and then I can get some sleep before your Pa gets back.'

Ray didn't know what to say. It seemed like there were two truths – the one you said out loud and the one that you held in your own head. She knew Ma looked sick and way more than tired. She tried picturing herself in that chair, working the herbs. Would she look a grey husk of a woman too? She couldn't see it. She just couldn't see herself at all. Every time she closed her eyes, all she saw was an empty chair.

'Ma, here give me the stone. I'm done with the candles. I can finish that, and you can go lay your head down, get some sleep.' Ray stood and carefully took the bowl from Ma's hands. Ma looked up and smiled. For a moment, there was an electric shock as their eyes met and Ray saw the woman that she could be. Or maybe she saw the woman that her Ma had once been. But in an instant, it was gone. Ma was heading toward the small room at the back of the cabin, head bowed, shoulders slumped.

Ray woke a few hours later to the sound of men's voices forcing their way in through the shutters. The fire had burned down. The cabin was dimly lit by slits of moonlight sliding through the shutters and the embers smouldering in the fireplace. She rose from her sleeping mat in front of the fire and peered out through the shutters. She could see the full moon and shapes of men and horses outside.

'Ma,' she hissed as she grabbed Pa's rifle as it stood, like a sentry, by the door. She gripped it with both hands to stop herself shaking, and called out again, louder, 'Ma, quick, we got trouble'. Her heart pounded in her chest, so hard she could hear it hammering in her ears. She backed up against the wall, squeezed her eyes shut and tried to slow her breathing. Ma appeared as a ghost, her hair a crackling halo in the dim half-light. She approached Ray, reaching out to gently take the rifle from her.

'Stay inside child,' she rasped, 'and keep away from the window'. She walked slowly to the door.

As Ma stepped outside, she solidified, her back straightened and she held her head high. She held the rifle in both hands, the barrel pointing toward the men and horses. Ray peered out of the shutters. She could make out three men seated on horseback and one man, barrel-tied over the back of his horse.

'What business have you got on my land this time of night?' Ma's voice rang out, sounding strong and fearless.

Silence.

One man got off his horse and walked slowly toward her, his arms away from his sides, signalling no threat. Ray could hear his muffled footsteps and the clinking of his spurs in the quiet night. When he was ten feet away, Ma called out. 'That's about far enough now'. She spoke calmly.

The man stopped and raised his hands in the air. They were empty, his gun still holstered. Of the other two, seated on their horses, one had a rifle resting easy in his hand, the barrel laid across his horse's neck. Ray's eyes darted between them. Fear rendering her weak and disconnected.

The man standing spoke. His voice was deep and slow; his words rolled carefully toward the cabin.

'Now, Ma'am, we're sorry to be bothering you at this time of night. We ain't looking for trouble, but sadly, this here business can't wait until morning. My name's Sheriff Boone, and I have a badge right here. I can show you if you'd allow me to put my hands down without getting a bullet for my troubles.'

Ma nodded. The man dropped his hands slowly and reached into the top pocket of his waistcoat. He pulled out a sheriff's badge, the moonlight glancing off the gold coating. Ma nodded once in recognition. He replaced the badge in his waistcoat, movements slow and careful.

'Now Ma'am, there was some bad business in town tonight and I'm told that this here man is your husband.' He gestured behind him, and one of the horsemen let go of the riderless horse. It walked slowly past the Sheriff toward the cabin, head lowered as if in mourning. Ray recognised the small star on its forehead and the two white socks at the front. It was Pa's horse. It walked on, past the cabin, toward the barn. As it passed her, Ma glanced at the body slung across its back. She turned back to face the Sheriff, her face a blank mask.

'Well, yes I believe that is my husband.'

The Sheriff nodded his head, placing one hand reverentially on his chest.

'Ma'am I am sorry for your loss. Your man was drinking hard in the saloon tonight, and fair to say, he was mighty soaked. He got to shooting his mouth off leading to some difficulty with Rancher Jared Mickleton. I guess you know him? He's a neighbour of yours, lives just over yonder, past your fence line. I'm told one minute it was words, the next it was on the street, guns drawn. Your man shot first, got the other fella in the leg, then he took a bullet in the chest. He died before he hit the ground. There was no suffering, if that's any comfort to you Ma'am. Rancher Mickleton bled out on the ground from that leg shot. Doc tried but couldn't save him. It's a bad business, that's for sure.'

He paused, still looking at Ma. The silence hung heavy in the air. Ray's breathing rasped, echoing in her ears. She felt suspended, frozen, as if she had become detached from the earth. The man's words were still floating outside of her as she tried to make sense of them. After a few seconds, the man spoke again.

'The thing is, Ma'am, plenty of folks in the saloon stand to the fact that your man started this altercation and that he drew his gun first. Rancher Mickleton's oldest boy was there in town and sad to say he saw his Pa bleed out, right there in the dirt. He tells me that this whole sorry affair started because your man owes them money. Seems like he hired the Mickleton's plough and horses at the beginning of the season but never paid. Seems like he promised to pay once the crops came in, but on account of the drought there ain't been no crops to harvest. I'm told that Rancher Mickleton offered to take some of your land for grazing in place of the money, but your man didn't take to that idea.'

Silence fell again. Ma stood rigid in front of the cabin. The rifle still clutched in her hands, loose now, hanging. She looked small and frayed in contrast to the Sheriff. His shadow, dark and heavy, stretched tall in front of him, falling at Ma's feet. He tipped his hat back on his head, as if to see Ma more clearly. Ray watched his shoulders rise and fall with a sigh she couldn't hear.

'Ma'am I am truly sorry for your loss, but I'm also sorry to say that the issue of the debt owed hasn't died with your husband. I believe that Dwain Mickleton may well be calling at your door looking to get that debt paid. That is his right, and I'm expecting that he'll be polite and respectful in his calling. And if that's not the case you be letting me know.'

And with that, they were gone.

There were no more words, just the sound of hooves retreating into the night.

Pa dead. Ma fading away before her eyes. A debt to pay. Ray stood motionless, frozen in time. It was too much to take in. Her thoughts, fractured and scattered, swirled around her.

The future felt as dark as the night sky.

Two

Pa was committed to the earth. No ceremony, no tears, just toil. The ground was iron-hard. By the end of the day's digging, Ray's arms and hands tingled and her muscles jittered. Her eyes stung from the salty sweat that encrusted her face. Ma wheezed and coughed. The sun dropped out of the sky, as Ray fashioned a crude cross of firewood and carved Pa's name into it. All her life he'd just been Pa, it was funny she'd never thought of him by his name and never would. They stood silently by the grave. Exhaustion, sadness and despair left them bereft of words. But their absence caused a heaviness in the air. As they paused, each with their own thoughts, Ray glimpsed the mound of a second grave next to Pa's. She blinked and it was gone, leaving her skin shivering.

Ma poured them a cup of coffee with a splash of Pa's whiskey. They sat on the veranda of the cabin watching the moon rise in the clear night sky.

'Ma, what's going to happen now?'

Ma gave no answer. Because there was no answer. All that lay ahead was uncertainty and trouble. Ray felt Ma's pain as clearly as if she'd spoken it out loud, and it nipped at her insides. Ma, gazing at the horizon, said softly:

'Sally, Jared Mickleton's wife, I ain't seen her in a long few years. She's been stuck away on that ranch, standing by Jared's side in spite of everything. In spite of him. Maybe she still loves him, maybe not. I don't know, but Pa might just of done her a favour, even if she don't know it to be true.'

Ma laughed at her own words. The laughter turned to coughing, then hacking, her chest heaving, her body coiling in on itself. Ray waited quietly for Ma to continue.

'The Mickleton's came out here before the rest of us, y'know. They set themselves up good and proper making money from hiring out their plough and team. Built their place off the backs of everyone else, then turned to cattle. They was the first people round here to get steers, taking up homesteads as they fell vacant. Then they built a fence round their land like they was creating their own kingdom. They've had their eyes on this place ever since.' She shook her head. 'Seems like they'll be coming for it now.'

Ma took a deep wheezing breath, then set to coughing uncontrollably.

Her cough sounded rotten like she'd dredged it up from the stinking ground. Ray could hear the mud gurgling in her lungs. She was tired and grey, her edges becoming blurred. And too often, there was a look on Ma's face like she was someplace else. Ray hoped it was somewhere better.

Ray and Ma sure weren't cut from the same cloth. She stood more than a head taller than Ma. Her long limbs contrasted with Ma's stockiness. She was even as tall as Pa, although she didn't look like him neither. In her twenty years, Ray had only been to town a handful of times, but she thought everyone in town looked much the same, and much like Ma and Pa. White folks with brown hair, brown skin from dirt and sun, and dull brown eyes. All looking like they're holding onto life with the tips of their fingers. When they smiled the dust left white creases. It was like the smiles were cracking their faces. Ray was different. She had red hair, just as red as the sun when it peeked over the mountains in the morning. Her hair was thick and wiry and nothing she could do could tame it to her head. Her eyes were pale blue, and her skin was so white that not even the hot sun could darken it.

For a day or two after they buried Pa, Ma seemed to look a little better, she smiled a bit more and her eyes looked brighter. But it was short-lived. The days after she stayed in bed a bit longer, coughed a bit more and seemed to shrink into herself. Ray worked from dawn till dusk and then some, as if through hard work she could quiet the constant worry gnawing in her belly. At night she slept on a mat in front of a cooling hearth. She dreamt of a land on fire, the cries of horses and the shrill screams of ravens heralding the troubles to come.

It was late one hot afternoon, she was feeding and watering the horses in the barn, when she heard the muffled clump of hooves in the dirt, the gentle tinkling of spurs and the flapping of leather chaps. She knew it was the Mickleton brothers. Every day, she'd woken dreading they'd turn up. Every day they hadn't, she'd felt relief, but an ever-growing tension. She grabbed the pitchfork, taking a deep breath. And with only the slightest of tremors, she walked out of the barn.

She raised her hand, signalling them stop. She guessed the one at the front was Dwain, the older brother. A hint of a smile appeared on his face before he spoke.

'Well, well, you must be Ray.' His voice was rough, as if the words were coated in sand. Dwain smiled at Ray and looked as relaxed as if he was visiting for Sunday supper. Pete, the younger, sat slightly behind, avoiding looking at her. He wasn't smiling. Dwain dismounted. He was moving slowly and keeping his hands where she could see them. Pete followed behind, as if he didn't want to be too close to his brother.

'I'm Dwain Mickleton.' He gestured behind him. 'And I believe you've met my brother Pete. Seems like we have some things to talk about now that our Pa's are gone. Is your Ma about?' Dwain looked around taking in the cabin and the barn. Ray remained still and silent. Her breath a hard knot in her chest.

'You've lost your Pa, and we all know that your Ma is sick. And we got this issue of your Pa's debt to consider. We just want to do the neighbourly thing and figure out how we can reach a kind of ...' he paused, looking for the right word, '...accommodation.'

Ray glanced at the cabin door hoping that Ma would appear and take charge. She felt like she was made of dust, loose and fleeting. It took all her energy to stand still and hold the pitchfork upright. She forced herself to open her mouth and willed the words to form.

'Me and Ma are doing just fine, but we thank you for your concern. I don't know about no debt, except what the Sheriff said. Seems to me like we don't got nothing to give you except our sympathies that you lost your Pa.'

Dwain crossed his arms over his chest. His smile still there, but with no softness behind it. He glanced at Pete; he waved his arm in an all encompassing gesture.

'Well, we're mighty glad you're managing now,' he said pointedly, 'but this here's a lot for two women to manage for more than just a few weeks, 'specially in this drought, crops dying. It's hard times, I'll say that. And as for the debt, well see the thing is

Ray, that your Pa killed our Pa. Murdered him right in the street over an argument and a debt he owed. Without our plough and horses, your Pa would never have planted those crops out there. And now we need...'

Dwain turned to Pete. 'What's it we need there, Pete?'

Pete turned to Ray before answering. He spoke softly, as if the words made him sad.

'Restitution, Dwain, that's the word you're looking for – restitution.'

'That's right, Ray,' continued Dwain. 'We're just looking for restitution.'

Ma appeared at the cabin door.

'You hush yourselves,' she said. I'm not in no mood to be discussing this today'. Ray breathed relief at the sound of Ma's voice. She felt herself solidify and slowly let out the breath she'd been holding, seemed like forever.

Dwain turned to face Ma. He looked solid, strong and confident. He wasn't a tall man but was thick set and powerful. His square jaw set rigidly in place like he was issuing a permanent challenge. Ray could feel the tension coming off him, making the air thick and heavy.

He spoke slowly and clearly, words hard and hollow. 'Ma'am, we are sure sorry for your loss, and we hope that you're not feeling too poorly. Your man told us you had the consumption, and we all know where that leads. We just want to do the neighbourly thing and make sure that you and your girl here are fine, and along the way we'll be getting what we're owed.'

Ma replied, 'Thank you for your concern, young Dwain. You can pass on our condolences to your Ma.' She paused, letting her words settle, before continuing. 'Now, I know the homestead owes you for the plough and you'll get your money when the time is right. My man told your Pa you'd get that money when the crop comes in and he accepted those terms. I don't see no crops and don't see no need to change them terms right now.'

Ma's words held in the air for a second or two then floated towards the hills, leaving silence in their wake. Dwain smiled at Ma and turned toward Ray where his gaze lingered a little longer, looking her slowly up and down.

'Thing is Ma'am we all know where this drought is heading. It ain't likely there'll be a harvest less we get some rain. Besides, now our Pa is gone we're a man short over the ranch, so we'll be needing to hire in some extra help, and that costs money.'

Ray watched as Pete took a step forward and placed his hand on Dwain's shoulder, his lips grazing Dwain's ear as whispered words passed between them. Dwain nodded slowly before tipping his hat at Ma.

'Ma'am, I guess you'll still be feeling the shock from the loss of your man, and you might not be thinking real clear. So we'll be on our way, but just for now. You take some time and have a think on this here situation. We'll come by again soon to talk some more on the matter.'

Ray watched as Dwain languidly mounted his horse. 'Just one last thing before we go Ma'am. We wanted to let you know there's some neat little rooms going at the White House in town. Would sure be a nicer place for you with the sickness, and no outdoor work to ruin your girl.'

He turned back to rest his gaze on Ray.

'She could make easy money too, just lying on her back. She's sure got a strange look about her. But I'm sure there's plenty that wouldn't mind, and she'd get some customers.'

Unsmiling, Dwain reined his horse around and rode off without a backwards glance. Pete threw a look at Ray. Their eyes locked briefly. Then he too turned his horse and was gone.

Three

5 years ago:

Ray stood in the barn, breathing in air sweet with the smell of horses. This felt like home. Their needs were uncomplicated, and she understood them, just as she felt they understood her. She hummed as she worked, immersion in the simple tasks bringing a sense of calm, allowing unwanted thoughts to drift away. As she turned to stow an empty bucket she heard a cough. Looking up she saw a young man leaning casually against the open barn door. His hat was tipped back on his head, his arms folded across his chest. As he watched her a faint smile spread across his face.

'Who are you? What do you want?' Ray blurted out. The words were sharp, holding panic at their edges. She clutched the handle of the bucket tighter, edging closer to Rio.

The man raised his hands as though to convince her he was no threat.

'Hey girl, relax,' he said softly. 'My name is Pete Mickleton, my family has the ranch just over yonder. My Pa sent me over. We need some extra hands for branding, and he wondered if your Pa was looking for some work?'

He smiled and left the question hanging.

'My Pa's off in town right now with Ma, picking up supplies.' The words came out in a rush. She took a gulp of air, trying to slow her breathing. She turned her head away before speaking again. The words came slower this time. 'So, you'll probably have to come back another time to ask him.'

Ray was fearful. Ma and Pa rarely had visitors out to the homestead and she wasn't used to strangers. People unsettled her. This man standing at her barn door made her nervous. He seemed relaxed and calm. She felt jittery, like a bird, eager to spread its wings and swoop out the barn door. She started when he began to slowly walk toward her. Eyes wide, she watched each step.

'Well, that's a fine pony you have there,' he said gently, with his eyes on Rio.

As he got closer Ray could smell him. He wasn't like Pa; all sour with sweat and cigars. He smelt sweet like the horses. He petted Rio, who stood calm and still under his touch. He turned to smile at Ray; their eyes were level when they met.

'Why girl you sure are tall. Here we are eye to eye and I'm six feet tall dammit.' A smile lit up his face. 'And that hair of yours, well I ain't never seen hair that colour. It sure is just like the sun coming up'.

Ray's heart clamped in her chest. His closeness felt alien. Blood was rushing in her ears. Her eyes widened as he extended a hand to her. She wanted to move but froze as he gently stroked her hair.

'Well ain't that something,' he said with a smile. 'Your hair is soft as a foal's mane.'

He took a step back and the spell was broken. When he spoke again it was as if the moment had never happened.

'I'm interested to talk to your Pa about the work, so I'll come by another day.'

Then he turned and walked back out of the barn without a backwards glance. Ray stood fixed to the spot. As he moved out of sight she exhaled deeply and leant onto Rio. There was comfort in his familiar warmth.

It was a week or so before Pete returned to the homestead, this time Pa was home. He paid no attention to Ray. He was polite to Ma, but spent his time talking to Pa about the ranch. And what work there might be if Pa was interested. They talked horses, and land, and guns, and at the end he tipped his hat to Ray and Ma and rode away. Ray felt something when he left. In her confusion, she didn't realise it was disappointment.

Ray thought about Pete in the weeks that followed. As Pa rode off to the ranch each morning, for the few weeks of paid work, she was reminded of the tall young man. It wasn't long before he came by the homestead again. She came out of the cabin to meet him and noticed that he was holding a small sprig of wildflowers.

'Well howdy there miss, you'd be the person I want to see,' he said as he dismounted and approached, pushing the flowers toward her.

'Go on, take them,' he said. I saw them in the lee of the hill on my way back from town and thought I'd pick them for you.'

Ray took the flowers. She could feel herself getting hot and red about the face, tension creeping into her limbs.

'They sure are pretty, thank you,' she said shyly.

'Well, they are pretty, that's for sure, and it's only right they're for you, cos you sure are pretty too.'

Ray and Pete stood looking at each other for a few more seconds, Pete smiling confidently and Ray looking anxious and unsure. Then with a tip of his hat Pete turned and got back on his horse.

'I'll be seeing you again very soon girl.'

'My name is Ray,' she mumbled as Pete rode away.

Four

Days seemed to merge into one as if time wasn't passing at all. The sun rose quickly in the morning and stood like a burning sentinel jealously guarding the barren land. When there was a breeze, dust rose and fell, making patterns in the air, forming creatures of light and dirt to follow Ray as she worked. The relentless heat lasted until the sun dropped behind the distant hills leaving only a dark silence. Without the sun, the earth lost its warmth and a chill rapidly descended. The moon's arrival birthed a whole new world where fear walked the earth unchecked.

As darkness fell, Ray finished sorting out the horses in the barn and made her way back to the cabin. Ma had prepared food. They ate in silence, full of exhaustion and laden with unspoken words and thoughts.

Ray watched Ma's every mouthful. In the weeks since Pa's death, she'd become frailer, her features shrinking and sinking into her skull. Wisps of grey hair floated round her face.

'You have it girl,' she said softly, as she scraped the remainder of her meal into Ray's bowl. 'I'm not hungry and you're doing the work of two men. You need the food.'

She shuffled off to wash her bowl. Ray watched slyly. Despite her tottering steps there was strength in Ma's back, and she still held her head high. Ray wondered if she was functioning on sheer pride and strength of will alone.

Ma turned to Ray and smiled.

'I'll just lay my head for a bit girl,' she said.

She made her way to the room at the back of the cabin and collapsed into her cot. Ray could hear her laboured breathing — the sound of pain and exhaustion. Air forcing its way through tortured lungs. Ray wondered how long Ma had left. She wondered how long either of them had left. One thing Dwain had said was true — they couldn't manage the homestead by themselves. Not like this and not for much longer.

The next morning Ray woke at dawn to silence and a feeling of panic. She jumped up and ran into Ma's room. She seemed frozen, lying with her back facing Ray, her body curled up tight like a small child. Ray felt fear bubbling up inside her. Her limbs shook and breath caught in her throat.

Oh God! Please no, not Ma.

Fearfully, she reached out.

'Ma,' she said softly, then louder. 'Ma!' her voice rising in panic, as she touched Ma's shoulder. She was still warm. With Ray's other hand she felt her breath, faint, warm and damp against her palm.

Thank God, thank God.

'Ma!' she called, louder now, gently shaking her shoulder. Ma uttered a small groan, but didn't open her eyes. Ray pulled up the blanket, tight under her chin, and smoothed her hair, whispering, 'It's ok Ma, I'm going to ride into town and get the Doc. You're going to be fine. We'll just get you some medicine and you'll be fine.'

Ray saddled Rio with shaking hands. The pony was too small for her, not as fast as Pa's gelding, but she trusted him. And right now, that trust meant everything. As the seconds passed, Ray felt panic building. What would she do if Ma died? How could she cope on her own? What would happen to her? But there was no time to think about that now. With legs as weak as saplings, she led Rio out of the barn, gathered her skirts and mounted. Leaning forward in the saddle, she flicked her reins, urging the pony to gallop toward town.

Ray arrived in billowing clouds of dust, as if she were a whole posse. She came to a stop outside the Doc's office. Ignoring the looks of bystanders, she climbed the steps two at a time and pushed through the door.

'Doc, you there?' she called, eyes darting around the waiting room. The pretty young receptionist sat quietly composed behind a desk, a smile pasted on her face.

'Ma'am, please don't be shouting in the Doctor's office.'

Rising, she smoothed the front of her dress. Her light brown hair was curled and pinned, her pale blue dress both professional and womanly. She stared at Ray, exuding an aura of calm dignity.

'I need the Doc, I think my Ma's dying,' Ray croaked, throat parched from the ride. The receptionist glided toward the Doctor's treatment room.

'Who shall I say is poorly?' she asked, raising an eyebrow. Ray felt her disapproval of her trail-dust appearance.

'My name's Ray and my Ma Lena is dying. She's got the consumption. Doc knew my Pa too.' She blurted, feeling her voice catch and tears pricking the corner of her eyes.

The Doc strode out of his office, a figure of calm authority. He wore a three-piece suit. His belly strained the buttons, and a gold watch chain looped across the front. He had a kind face, and his eyes were soft with concern when he took in Ray's appearance. Her slim six-foot frame topped by her long red hair fizzing out from under her hat. The ragged and patched brown dress, her work boots sticking out underneath. The whole of her covered in a fine layer of brown dust dulling her skin but making her pale eyes seem even brighter.

'It's my Ma, please you've got to come and help my Ma, I think she's dying', she pleaded, her hands clutching at the rough fabric of her dress.

The Doc nodded slowly. 'Ok, keep yourself calm, I'll come and see your Ma. To be honest, I've been expecting it', he said kindly. He turned to the lady in the blue dress. 'Please my love, can you get one of the boys to hitch up the buggy and I'll go pay Lena a visit.'

After he had collected his bag, and his horse was hitched to the buggy, Ray and the Doc rode out of town toward the homestead. Ray chafed at the slow pace. She had to force Rio to walk alongside. Her mind raced ahead to what they might find back at the homestead.

The Doc turned toward Ray with a kind smile as if he could read her mind.

'There ain't no need to rush with what ails your Ma,' he said, before lapsing back into silence. The horses' hoofs played out a tune on the hard packed earth. Ray and the Doc continued their way slowly under the hot sun to the homestead. As they crested a small hill, Ray could see their place up ahead, the barn and the small cabin just to the side of it. On the south side of the acreage, she thought one of the fences was down between her place and the Mickleton's, but it was difficult to tell, and her mind was on more important things.

When they eventually arrived, Ray watered the horses whilst the Doc went inside to see to Ma. After she'd finished tending to the animals she paced up and down the veranda, waiting for the Doc to emerge. Eventually he came out to join her, wiping his hands and forehead with a large spotted handkerchief.

'Ray, I'm afraid I don't have any good news for you', he said gently. 'Your Ma is dying, in fact I'm surprised that she hasn't let go by now, but it won't be long.' He gestured toward one of the veranda chairs whilst easing himself down into the other. He waited for Ray to sit before continuing.

'I've made your Ma comfortable, and I've left you something that you can give her if she becomes distressed or seems in pain. But I'm afraid that you're just going to have to wait until her mind decides it's had enough. Now that might be in an hour or two, or it might be a few days yet, but I don't think much longer than that. Now, when she goes you can get her brought into town for a proper burying if you want, or you can bury her here. But you need to tell me when she's gone, so I can make a note of it for the town records.'

Ray sat in silence, with the Doc's words drifting in the dust just out of reach. Fear shrouded her, dulling her senses. She nodded to the Doc. She felt loose and unconnected, like she might just break apart and join the swirling dust caught in the breeze cooling the veranda. The Doc leaned across and patted Ray's leg.

'Now I don't know what you'll do when your Ma dies?' He looked around taking in the homestead. 'You can't run this land by yourself, grow the corn, keep wood on the fire. You'll need to get some help, or sell up and move into town.'

Ray shook her head. She couldn't find the words, but she knew she wouldn't be leaving the homestead. It was the only home she'd ever known. She didn't fit in town and she didn't think she'd be welcome. And what would she do for money? She didn't know what she was going to do, but she figured she'd rather die on her land, and be buried with Ma and Pa, than leave it.

Ray spent the next few days floating around the cabin and the barn in a daze waiting for Ma to pass on. She spent hours sitting by her bed listening to her laboured breathing and administering medicine when the pain came bad. She ate next to nothing and let the homestead look after itself. Her only respite was the time she spent in the barn caring for the horses. Breathing in their comforting smell and stroking the soft hair on their bodies, she could almost forget everything going on around her. For those brief moments she felt safe and whole. Then she'd take a deep breath and go back inside, nurse Ma, and sit quietly, listening to the rattle of her breathing.

Ma was there. And then a moment later, she wasn't. It was so quick and so quiet that Ray couldn't believe it had happened. One minute Ray was listening to the broken rhythm of strained breath escaping from Ma's lips, and the next minute there was nothing but silence. No wind, no birds, no creaking of the cabin's joints and no breath. Just silence and stillness. For a second, Ray felt a peace flow over her and tension flake off her skin. But then she felt a pain in her chest and heard herself making sharp keening sounds, as if she were listening from elsewhere. She laid her head on Ma's chest and tears flowed from her eyes, as she wept for her Ma and for her lost life. Ray didn't know how long she spent laying against Ma, but as coldness settled into Ma's bones, it flowed into Ray. She felt the chill of loneliness and fear.

Ray buried Ma out the back of the barn, next to Pa. It took her most of two days to get the hole dug and make the cross. The ground, baked hard by the sun, felt like digging iron. By the time she'd finished, her arms and shoulders burned and her back felt so stiff she thought she'd break in two when she stood up straight. She had to lay Ma on a blanket to drag her out of the cabin. At the makeshift grave she rolled Ma up in the blanket and pushed her shrouded body into the ground. As she heard the thud of Ma hitting the hard dirt below, she began to shake so hard she felt she would shatter into a thousand pieces. Her whole body was awash with pain and the tears came so fast she could barely see to shovel dirt onto Ma's body.

Ma was really gone.

Ray collapsed with exhaustion on top of the grave. She was dry of tears, but full of pain and fear. Her head spun and she squeezed her eyes tight, feeling a small part of herself break free and rise up into the evening air. She could see herself from above curled up on top of the grave, like a discarded bundle of rags. She looked like a broken thing, no good to anyone. Her free spirit drifted further up, until she was just a speck below. It whirled and twisted on the wind, helpless to its fate but content to let the wind take it. It looked down on hills and mountains, rivers and streams, and small towns of wood and dirt. She saw the world of men slashed across the landscape and the insignificance of it all.

When Ray woke, it was dark outside with clouds obscuring the moon and the chill night air seeping into her bones. She managed to crawl off Ma's grave and hobble across to the cabin. With hands still shaking, she lit the fire. Sitting as close as she dared, she warmed slowly. Her blistered hands and aching body reminding her Ma was gone.

She was alone.

Five

The silence in the cabin was as deep and empty as Ray's heart. She stood alone, hollow with loss, taking in her surroundings. The worn wooden furniture was made smooth through use. The sod floor, swept so often, it was now as hard and black as coal. The fireplace, once a symbol of the warmth of her small home, now cold with last night's embers, grey and still.

It was time to make a trip into town. Supplies were low, and she needed to tell the Doc about Ma. Ray had found a small bag of coins under the mattress when she'd cleaned up after Ma's death. She suspected Ma had been taking coins from Pa when he was drunk, so he didn't gamble everything away. Finding them had given Ray a little hope. She might be able to hold onto the homestead for a while longer. Her gaze caught the rifle propped up in its usual place by the door. Without thinking, she picked it up, feeling the warmth and smoothness of the wood. It felt comforting and alive in her hands. Then she remembered Pa's Colt that she'd thrown in the trunk with the rest of his things. She grabbed that too, tucking it into the waistband of her skirt, before heading out the door.

The ride into town with the wagon was slow. The ground hard and pitted with small rocks, every bump jarring, building her anxiety. She knew that once she told Doc Ma was gone, it wouldn't be long before the news got out to the Mickleton's. When Dwain knew she was alone at the homestead, she didn't know what he might do.

She parked the wagon by the general store. She hitched Pa's gelding to the rails and headed down the main street to the Doc's office. As she got closer, she could see him standing on the veranda, smoking a cigar alongside another man. A tall, slim man with a black Stetson, and spurs glinting off the back of his fancy tooled boots.

Ray came level with the veranda looking up at the Doc. She didn't like that he was looking down on her, so walked on a little and up the steps to join him. She faced him, eye to eye, ignoring the other man, breaking the silence by answering his unspoken question.

'Ma passed away. I've buried her on our land next to Pa.' Sadness and loss were held in the simplicity of Ray's words. The Doc watched her carefully, noting the tension she carried in her shoulders, and the twitching of her fingers as she stood facing him.

'I sure am sorry for your loss, Ray', he spoke gently, reaching out to touch her lightly on the arm, hoping to offer some comfort. She flinched at his touch. He spoke again, his voice soft with concern, 'How are you doing girl?'

'I'm ok', answered Ray. She stood as straight as she could, squaring her shoulders. She looked the Doc in the eye, challenging him to disagree with her.

The tall man watched the exchange, his features impassive. He stepped towards Ray. He was taller than her and up close his face was heavily lined, but his features were clean and strong. He took in Ray's appearance. She stood tall, rifle slung over her shoulder. Her mass of red hair, unwashed and unbrushed for days, was matted, and poured out from under her hat like a lava flow. Dishevelled and dirty she may be, yet her pale blue eyes shone.

'I don't know if you remember me, Ray. I'm Sheriff Boone.'

He paused, waiting for a sign of recognition, but she remained silent, expressionless. He sighed, wondering how he could get through to this ragged girl in front of him. He felt like he was standing in front of a wild horse, hoping she wouldn't spook. He pushed away the unwanted thought, and continued:

'Girl, you and I need to have a talk. I've had young Dwain Mickleton come by a day or so ago, saying he is mighty worried for you.'

Ray tensed, her breath quickening.

'He ain't got no concern for me Sheriff, only thing he's concerned about is my land.'

'Now Ray, I ain't got no reason but to take Dwain Mickleton at face value. But this here issue of the debt...'

'There ain't no debt', interrupted Ray, anger in her voice. 'There's just a business arrangement. When my crops come in, I'll be paying back what's owed. That's the arrangement, that's what my Ma said.'

'Ray, I think we all know this drought is killing the crops, and Dwain's entitled to his payment. There's no conspiracy here girl, just a legal matter and some concern from your neighbours, as to your well-being and safety.'

Ray shook her head. She could feel anger flowing through her, filling her with fire. She welcomed it, as it pulsed through her, washing away her fear and grief. She spoke like she was spitting bullets.

'You're wrong Sheriff. There ain't no concern for me. All that family want is our land. They wanted it, as long as I can remember. Making offerings to my Pa, but he always said no. The deal is when the crops come in. No crops, no deal.'

The Sheriff watched her. Anger radiated off her in waves and her eyes burned, pale and startlingly bright. There was a hard set to her mouth, and he thought she looked just this side of crazy. He shook his head. There was nothing he could say now that would make her see sense. He had no idea how this situation would play out, but he had a bad feeling that it wasn't going to go easy.

Ray let her gaze slide off the Sheriff. She nodded a goodbye to the Doc, before turning and walking carefully back down the steps off the veranda. She moved through town, flooded with emotion, doing what she had to do, collecting supplies. Her skin tingled and her shoulders ached with tension. She tried to ignore the sideways glances of the townsfolk, and the way they moved out of her way when she passed them. She felt different from these people. She looked different from these people. They were like cattle — monochrome and tethered to the earth. She shrugged off their murmuring voices and pitying looks, straightened her back and lengthened her stride — her anger giving her strength.

Her final stop was at the hardware store to pick up bullets for Pa's guns. The store was full of men and chatter when Ray walked in. Cowboys chewing and talking fell silent when they found Ray standing in their midst.

'How can I help you, Miss?', called out the storekeeper, beckoning her closer to the counter.

'I need shells for my rifle and this pistol,' demanded Ray, taking the Colt and placing it on the counter. The storekeeper checked to make sure it wasn't loaded.

'You need to be careful with this Missy, you don't want to hurt nobody by accident — or yourself.'

Ray stood in silence.

The storekeeper continued as if he didn't expect a response.

Pointing at the rifle, he said, 'I see you're carrying Melvin's Winchester. You must be his girl. I heard about your Pa. I'm sorry for your loss.'

The silence continued with no response from Ray. The storekeeper placed several boxes of shells on the counter.

'That's a fine rifle. I remember when Melvin won it in a poker game straight off some high-brow traveller in a fancy suit. Old Melvin fancied that inlaid stock, and he sure played a mean game of cards to get it. Fella wasn't happy handing it over, but he lost it fair and square.'

The storekeeper chuckled inwardly at the memory. Ray silently handed over coins and grabbed the boxes, before striding out past the chittering cowboys. Their words followed her as she left the store.

'I heard Melvin kept her out there on his land cos she's crazy…'

'Hell, she looks like a child of the devil that one…'

'Yeah, I heard they found her abandoned on the wagon trail, no one knows where she came from…'

By the time Ray got back to the homestead her rage had turned from fire running through her veins to a lump of cold lead in her gut. But the decision was made; she would be ready to protect herself and her land. She took the Colt and some shells out back of the cabin. Picking out some logs from the wood pile, she set one on top of a fence post. She loaded the Colt, took twenty paces back from the fence, turned and fired the pistol.

Shit, missed!

She took five paces forward, pointed and emptied the cylinder. Still nothing. She sighed, feeling the anger subsiding into anxiety and frustration.

'You weren't holding it right', a man's voice drawled from behind her. Ray spun round to see Pete Mickleton standing there, calm, smiling.

'Jesus, Ray, don't be pointing that gun at me,' he hissed, raising his hands in mock surrender. 'Don't expect you'll hit me on purpose, but you might just do it by mistake.'

Ray realised she was pointing the gun directly at Pete. She lowered her hands. 'What do you want? Did your brother send you here?'

'No, Ray, he didn't.' Pete lowered his hands and walked toward Ray. He looked sad, his eyes hooded, mouth turning down at the corners. He spoke gently as he came closer.

'Ray, I just wanted to come by and check you're ok. I know my brother's got you rattled about this debt, but he's not what you think. He's just trying to look out for the family, that's all.'

Ray didn't answer. She couldn't assemble her fragmented thoughts and express them in words. She stood silently in front of Pete, her eyes tracing the features of his face. A shadow passed between them and Ray looked up to see a raven, its sooty blackness swooping in lazy circles above her. She stood entranced by its lonely aerial dance.

'Hell, seeing as how I'm here, how about I show you how to shoot that thing?'

The spell was broken; Ray looked back toward Pete. Without speaking she handed him the gun.

Pete placed another log on top of the fence post and led Ray back twenty paces. He turned, took aim, and shot off five rounds, hitting the log every time and sending it flying off the top of the post. Smiling, he turned to Ray, held out a hand for more shells, and reloaded the cylinder. Then he balanced another log on the post.

'See, that's how you do it. Now let me show you.'

He passed the gun to Ray. With his hands on her shoulders, he gently turned her to face the target. Standing behind her, he reached around and gently placed his hands over hers on the grip. Then he raised it level with the target. Ray gulped in air, her body tensing. He stood so close she could feel his warm breath on her neck. Her mind screamed at her to push him away, but her body remained still. Her muscles began softening as her breath settled into the same rhythm as Pete's. She thought she'd faint when he nudged her legs apart with his knee.

'Widen your stance, you need to be firm on the ground.'

Ray's breath became light; she felt Pete's presence enfolding her. His voice came soft in her ear.

'Now, you just breathe a little slower, and you focus on nothing but the barrel of the gun and the target in front of you.'

He took his hands from hers.

'Now take yourself out the picture. It's just the gun and the target. Breathe slow and steady and when you're ready, take a little hold of that breath and squeeze the trigger.'

Ray squeezed the trigger and felt the shock waves from the gun travel up her arms and into her shoulders. Almost instantly she heard a thud, and saw the log topple from the fencepost. She breathed out and felt an instant of wonder — she'd hit her target. She'd need practice aplenty, but now she knew with time and patience she'd be able to shoot something if she needed — or someone.

'There you go, girl', said Pete gently, stepping away from her. Ray felt the absence of Pete's hands and warm breath. She felt the distance between them as a coolness; despite the heat of the sun, she shivered. Pete stood in front of her. The silence between them felt soft, unthreatening, until Pete began to speak.

'I know it's hard for you Ray, and I'm going to help in any way I can.'

He turned his gaze to the horizon; a frown on his face as he wrestled with his words.

'Thing is, this situation ain't good for nobody, not you and not my family. Now Pa's gone, Dwain's the head of the family and he's got to take care of everyone. Ma, me, and the ranch.'

Pete turned again to face Ray. Once more she saw sadness in his face.

'Truth is Ray, I'm not sure Dwain's ready for the weight of it. Our Pa was a tough son of a bitch, and he controlled everything and everyone at the ranch. Dwain's trying to do his best, and make the right decisions, but it's hard.'

Ray felt Pete's words. She felt their sorrow, and frustration. She felt a mix of emotions she couldn't untangle. She was acutely conscious of the man in front of her, feeling as if they were joined in some way, despite the distance between them. She felt the connection in her body, wanting to feel his warmth close to her again. But her reason rebelled.

He's a Mickleton, can I trust him?

The moment was broken.

'Ray, I got to head back to the ranch', he said, haltingly. 'You keep practicing with that gun, and the rifle too. I'll come back and look in on you in a while. In the meantime, you take care, you hear.'

Ray watched Pete walk back to his horse, with those long, smooth strides of his. Then her gaze drifted upwards to the solitary raven, still high in the sky, weaving its pattern. It let out a plaintive *caaaw,* as it disappeared from sight. When she brought her gaze back down, Pete had gone.

She was alone.

Again.

Six

Ray needed to hunt. It was her only option. She needed to get up into the hills and shoot herself some meat for the pot. Her survival depended on it. She was living on bread she'd made with the meagre remains of last year's corn. And bacon and beans that she'd bought in town. Daily she watched as her larder stocks diminished. There were still coins left, but they weren't going to last, and she doubted she could get work to earn more. The heat was relentless, the crops were wilting in the ground, and rain seemed a distant memory. Life felt hopeless. Too often, drifting off to sleep, she wished she wouldn't wake up to this miserable life.

Her anxiety grew as the days passed. She found herself gazing out from the homestead, longing to see the loping stride of Pete's mare approaching. She liked his company. She wasn't sure she could trust him, but he was the closest thing she had to a friend. His presence eased the disquiet that raged in her mind, fraying her edges. Instead, she talked to the horses. Caring for Rio and Pa's gelding gave her a reason to get up in the morning. In return they gave her comfort, and the warmth of living creatures. She realised that she still thought of their big bay gelding as Pa's horse. It was about time she gave him a name and made him hers. He was calm and gentle and had a kind nature. She decided to call him Rain, hoping it would be a prophecy.

That night was no different from the others. Yet with a surge of energy that came from nowhere, she spent the evening gathering everything she thought she might need to go hunting the next morning. She found Pa's old saddle bags and filled them with food, water and rifle shells. She packed a couple of blankets for the cold nights. She added matches, so she could light herself a fire and, on a whim, decided to pack herself a flask of whiskey. Then, Ray looked down at her skirt. She wore it all the time and hadn't washed it in weeks. It was filthy. She didn't think it would be good for hunting. Saw it getting all caught up on brambles and branches. Ray went into Ma and Pa's room. Hunting in their trunk, she found a pair of Pa's pants and put them on. At six feet tall, Ray was about the same size as Pa and they fitted well, if a little big round the waist. She found a belt to cinch them in and added one of Pa's waistcoats over the top of her shirt. She glanced down at herself and thought she'd do for hunting.

Next morning, at dawn, Ray holstered the loaded Colt, saddled Rain, put the saddle bags across his back and her rifle in the scabbard. Rio, her sure-footed friend, would have been her preference and she didn't want to be parted from him, but if she'd be bringing back meat, and hopefully plenty of it, Rain was bigger and stronger. She mounted up and rode out toward the hills, fear of the unknown jagging inside her. She glanced back at the cabin, just once, feeling the pull of home, the lure of the familiar. Nudging Rain to a canter, she forced herself away.

By the time she reached the base of the hills, the sun was high in the sky and her mouth was parched, her lips and nostrils coated in layers of dust. She let Rain pick his own way carefully across the rocky ground. She knew she'd have to stop soon and drink. Rain would need one too. She kept her eye on the hills ahead and the glimpses of shade filled pockets. It wasn't much longer before the ground started to ascend and huge boulders lined the trail casting long shadows between them. Ray found a shaded area and dismounted, her lower back and legs ached. She took deep gulps of water. Taking a pot from her saddle bag, she filled it with water for Rain. She figured she'd probably need to head a way further up into the hills, both to find game and a source of water.

Ray continued her journey following the trail as it climbed. She'd never ridden this far from the cabin before. The landscape around her felt outlandish. As she climbed higher the path narrowed. Jagged rocky outcrops replaced the rounded boulders, forcing her to continue upwards. She felt vulnerable on the narrow path, shadows flickered tricks in front of her eyes, and strange noises, scratching and rustling, came at her from all directions. A raven's plaintive call echoed in the space around her, but when she raised her eyes to the sky, it was nowhere to be seen. She felt as if she were being watched, the skin on her back tingled, but if there was someone, or something there, they remained hidden. She took comfort in the solidness of Rain. He plodded on, hoofbeats echoing in the narrow space, his body relaxed and his eyes on the path ahead. Then suddenly, they emerged into a new world, a world she had never known, a world a lifetime away from the brown dust of the homestead. All around her was green, thick bush, and big trees casting a soft, gentle shade. She felt the tension ebb away. As the sun was dipping low in the sky, she began looking for somewhere to camp.

It wasn't long before Ray came across a small clearing. The ground was trodden, and she could see hoofprints and the remains of a fire. She dismounted and tied Rain to a tree before kneeling and feeling the burnt earth. It was cold. She thought it had been a while since someone had camped here and she figured it would be safe enough. She removed Rain's saddle and left him to graze where he stood. Lush, green grass, unlike the short brown scrub of the homestead. It was cooler amongst the trees and as the sun continued its descent, she could feel it cooling further. She set about getting wood and kindling to light a fire before the chill of the evening set in.

After a meagre supper, she planned her hunt for dawn tomorrow. With weary eyes and an aching body, Ray leaned against a tree trunk and watched the fire. It looked as exhausted as she felt. Small wisps of orange snaked off the embers. They cast a low light trapping Ray on an island amidst the shadows cast by the trees and the moonlight. She felt truly alone in this place, away from the comforting walls of the cabin, and the ghosts of Ma and Pa. The trees and bushes, so welcoming when she arrived, looked sinister. She imagined the branches as spectral arms reaching for her. Breath rasped in her ears — tension invaded her body. She desperately wanted to close her eyes and sleep, but fear kept her wide awake. She was alert to the sounds of the woods: twigs snapping, leaves rustling, the grunts and calls of unseen creatures of the night. There were dangers here, she knew. Wild animals she didn't want to meet. Men. Men she didn't want to meet. So often, she wanted to close her eyes and not wake up in the morning. But now, here, amidst this strange world, she feared that very thing.

She took a mouthful of whiskey from Pa's flask. It should be her last, she needed to sleep. She drew the blankets round her, warding off the chill, wriggling to make herself comfortable. As her view lowered, shadows in the trees moved.

She froze.

Her heart stopped. Her breath caught in her throat. She strained her eyes in the dark, fear crawling through her. There it was again. Shadows moving, undergrowth parting. Her scalp tingled as slowly, so slowly, a man shaped shadow stepped out of the trees, creeping slowly toward her.

And there was nothing she could do.

Seven

Ray tasted iron on her tongue, nails pricked her scalp, her breath came like water was pooling in her lungs. With leaden limbs she reached slowly toward the rifle. It felt like the ground was shifting beneath her. Head spinning, she planted her hand on the dirt to stop herself tipping over — the shadow moved closer.

Her heartbeat louder drowning out the noise of the woods. The shadow left the darkness and the dim light from the dying fire caught a glimpse of red and gold braid. Red and gold? Cowboys and gold diggers don't wear red and gold, they drift in brown and grey, men of dirt and dust. The man approached slowly, gently, his aura relaxed and benign. A smile on his opening lips showed teeth white in the moonlight. His face was dark with a strong, broad nose and full lips. When he spoke, his voice was deep and soft and round. His words filled the space between them with warmth.

'Hey lady, you can pause on looking for that rifle, I don't mean you no harm. I'm just looking for the warmth of a fire.'

Ray watched, as he took another slow step forward, until all of him was cast in the dim firelight. A black hat framed a smiling face. He was shirtless and wearing a short black jacket lined with red and gold braid. The jacket was open, baring his dark chest to the chill of the night air. His tight black trousers were tied at the waist by a piece of rope. Standing patiently, he waited until Ray had recovered enough to give a small nod of her head.

Ray watched him warily as he settled cross-legged on the other side of the fire. He seemed foreign to her in his strange dress, but she realised she was no longer scared. She wondered why? Surely, she should be terrified being alone in the woods with a strange man. But somehow, she knew he wouldn't harm her.

After a few minutes, Ray spoke.

'I'm sorry, all the coffee's gone. You can have a sip of whiskey, if you'd like.' She leaned forward, offering the flask.

'I'm fine, thank you, ma'am,' the man replied. 'I'd just like the warmth of the fire and some company.' He articulated each word clearly and slowly and the sound of it felt soothing to her.

'Why don't you tell me what you're doing out here by yourself,' he continued.

Ray started to explain that she'd come out hunting. Before she knew it, she was talking non-stop about everything that had happened. Her Pa and then Ma dying, the struggle to keep the homestead going, and the debt with the Mickleton family. Ray found she couldn't stop talking. The words came out of her mouth of their own volition. A river of words flowing out of her, around the campsite and pooling at the feet of the strange looking man. As Ray spoke, he sat still and quiet, absorbing her words with a gentle smile on his face that told of understanding. As the words spilt out of her, Ray felt tension slipping from her shoulders and some of the tautness leaving her body. She felt her face soften and the hard lines of her mouth relaxing.

Eventually Ray paused for breath. She felt a small peel of laughter roll from her lips. Shaking her head, her eyes rolled up to the heavens.

'I don't know what just happened there, I don't usually talk much, specially to strangers. But it sure ain't very hospitable of me. You're sharing my fire, and I haven't asked your name.' She allowed the question to hang in the air.

'My name is Earl,' he said, tipping his hat toward her with a small bow.

'I'm pleased to meet you, Earl, I'm Ray. And it's a comfort to share my fire with you. Would you like one of my blankets?'

'I'll be fine,' he replied. I don't feel the cold too much, and I'll sit here with the fire for a bit longer.' He gestured toward her. 'Now perhaps you should rest your eyes, Ray. You got a big day tomorrow.'

As Ray closed her eyes to sleep, she wondered why the man would be out in the woods by himself. Maybe, she figured, he was travelling between towns, but that wouldn't explain why he was here alone. This and many other questions whirled around in Ray's head until eventually sleep took her.

Ray woke in the morning to a well-lit fire and Earl sitting calmly opposite, where he'd been the night before. She felt surprisingly well rested and after relieving herself and checking on

Rain, she set about making a pot of coffee. Whilst the coffee was brewing, she told Earl her plans for the day.

'I need to scout for animals. I'm hoping to hunt from this camp and maybe find some water, 'cos mine won't last much longer. I'd like to get some meat butchered and ready to take home tomorrow.'

'Would you like me to tag along?' asked Earl.

Ray caught flashes of colour from his coat. She hesitated before speaking, not wanting to hurt his feelings or seem ungrateful. But she wasn't sure he'd be at all helpful. More likely a hinderance. She couldn't afford this to be a wasted trip. Before she could frame the words Earl spoke:

'Don't let my appearance concern you. I have good sight, and I know how to track. It's no mean feat to take a life, even a jack rabbit. I think you might need my help.' He shrugged, before adding, 'and to be honest with you, I have nowhere else to be.'

Was he reading her mind?

Ray nodded. She felt comfortable with this man, despite only meeting him last night. Instead of her usual anxiety, she was reassured by his presence.

'Before we head out,' he said, 'you need a decent breakfast, so fix yourself some food and then we'll think about hunting.'

Ray put some bacon in a pan on the fire and tore off a hunk of bread to go with it. She hadn't brought much food with her. And she wondered if there would be enough to feed them both if she was out here for more than a day or two.

Earl stood, gesturing towards the woods.

'You go ahead and have your breakfast. I'll take a little scout around here and see if I can find some animal signs.'

With a smile, he walked toward the trees and within a second or two had disappeared into the woods. As he left the campsite, Ray felt his absence keenly. There was a slight chill in the breeze and she was aware once more of the sounds from the trees. She concentrated on frying the bacon and heating the last of the coffee.

After she'd eaten, Ray rinsed the pan out with a little of her water, rolled up her blankets and kicked some dirt over the fire to put it out. She gave a little water to Rain and then putting a knife in her belt and grabbing the rifle and some shells, she made to head into the woods.

'Ray!'

She spun round, startled by Earl's voice from behind her.

'We'll head this way,' he said, with softer tones. 'There's plenty of scat around here. Coyote, I think. We're a little low down for Bobcats. Jack rabbits too, plenty of them, but they're pretty hard to shoot. That means there'll be water nearby, too.'

They headed into the trees, with Earl leading the way. He walked slowly and carefully, his eyes scanning the ground for signs and, every now and then, stopping and looking around, as if he were sniffing the air. Ray followed blindly, trying to emulate Earl's careful steps as she made her way through the woods, to leave no trace of their passage.

Occasionally, Earl would raise a hand and point either left or right and they would move off in that direction. Ray felt they'd walked a long way, and she was unsure where she was in relation to her camp. She began to feel anxious, hemmed in by the trees, as she blindly followed the man in front of her. Then Earl held up his hand and they stopped. He turned and pointed to the ground in front of them, where Ray could see some faint small paw prints and then to the side, some droppings. Earl led them forward slowly between two large trees, until they came to a fallen tree with a small clearing on the other side of it. The air was still within the trees and Ray could hear her breathing and the small indistinct noises of life moving within the woods.

Earl motioned Ray to silence. They squatted behind the fallen tree. She rested the rifle barrel on the trunk and scanned the area in front of her. After a minute or two, she sensed Earl looking to his left and as her eyes moved across, she saw two small jack rabbit ears poking up between some bushes. She watched still and silent, as the ears moved closer into view and the jack rabbit stood, his nose twitching, as it scented the air.

Ray watched the jack rabbit down the barrel of her rifle. She felt the world shrink around her, conscious of nothing but the small creature. She focused on Pete's instructions to slow her breathing and focus on the gun and her target. Her finger was soft on the trigger ready to squeeze. The jack rabbit turned its head, its nose in the air until it was facing Ray. It appeared to look directly at her. She saw its eyes clearly, soft and bright brown. She imagined the bullet exploding from the barrel and entering its soft fur, ripping a black hole in burnt fur and blood and the light draining from the rabbit's eyes as it fell to the floor. She couldn't squeeze the trigger. In an instant the rabbit was gone.

Ray felt Earl's hand on her shoulder. She turned her head to see sorrow and understanding in his eyes. He was right, it wasn't going to be easy to take a life. Together they stood. Earl continued leading the way through the trees searching for other prey. After what felt like hours, once again Earl signalled Ray to stop. This time she found herself leaning against a tree looking down on a slope toward a small stream winding its way through the woods. Close to the water was another jack rabbit nibbling at some long slender leaves. Ray focused on the barrel of the rifle and the target in front of her. Breathing slow and steady, the world distilled down to this single moment. She felt Earl's hand squeeze her shoulder softly giving her courage and she squeezed the trigger. A spray of red fountained into the air and the rabbit slumped to the ground.

She collected the rabbit with a mix of feelings running through her. She was proud of her achievement; she couldn't quite believe she'd been able to hit the rabbit at all. In all her practicing with the rifle, she'd never been that accurate. She also felt a terrible sadness, as she looked at the lifeless body of the poor creature. It felt to her like the death of a child, a small black spot on the light of the world, a spot that would remain dark forever.

'You should tie it to your belt and then we'll carry on,' said Earl gently. 'One rabbit isn't going to feed you for long.'

He looked kindly at Ray, like he understood how she felt.

For the remainder of that day, Ray and Earl picked their way stealthily through the woods. Ray began to enjoy the environment, the sun sent dappled rays through the trees, and the coolness was a break from the relentless heat of the open ground of the homestead. She shot two more rabbits. Then stopped as a strange sound drifted through the air. Three or four staccato notes followed by a pause and then several more. Earl grasped Ray's hand and with an excited grin, he turned in the direction of the noise. After several minutes, Earl stopped and crouched. Ray could see a wild turkey ahead. The bird was huge. Ray watched fascinated as it stalked around, like it was lost. When she shot it turkey alarm calls filled the air.

Ray collected the carcass, surprised at the weight of it. She grasped it by the legs and threw it over her shoulder, it's warm bulk, a heavy reminder of the fragility of life. Without making comment, Earl turned and led the way back to camp. Ray followed; her heart was full of pride at the success of her hunt. She'd stepped out of the boundaries of the homestead, and she had survived. Much more than that, she'd ensured her survival, at least for a day or two. As she followed Earl, with his straight back and confident steps, she wondered how successful she'd have been without his help. She sure was grateful, but soon she'd be packing up her camp and heading back to the homestead, alone.

Eight

Ray was glad of Earl's presence. Darkness was falling around them. Alone she might have panicked, become disorientated, lost. Earl gave her confidence, as he sure-footedly led her back to camp.

Things were as they'd left them. Rain and her belongings were safe and well. Ray lit a fire and began the gruesome task of dressing her kill. She slit open each creature with her knife, using her fingers to strip out their guts. Their insides were still warm, even the rabbit she'd killed earlier that day. Ray felt she was removing their final link to life. As their plumped-up bodies deflated they were no longer animals, just meat and hides.

Ray was exhausted from the hours spent in the woods. She and Earl scarcely exchanged a word. When the work was done, she ate bread washed down with whiskey. She didn't have the energy to cook or even make coffee. She lay slumped against the tree trunk, wrapped in a blanket with the whiskey flask in her hand. She watched Earl, sitting cross legged opposite her, silhouetted by the fire. He sat, with his eyes closed, calm and still, at one with his surroundings despite his shining top hat and brightly braided coat. As weariness overtook her, through narrowed eyes she registered only the outline of the man in front of her. She saw the shapes of the trees behind, the leaves floating and flickering in the breeze. A small bird alighted from a branch and made its way in front of Earl, pecking at the ground for insects. It was soon joined by another, and another. Ray watched mesmerized as the birds ate their fill, seemingly oblivious to Earl's presence. She watched until exhaustion overtook her, and her eyes closed.

Ray woke to the sunrise, the early morning calls of the birds and Rain softly chomping the grass around him. The fire had burned out in the night. Ray threw off her blankets and started to light the fire to make breakfast. She was revitalised after a good sleep and starving after yesterday's efforts. She needed coffee before she started on the ride back to the homestead. It was only once she'd made breakfast, Ray remembered Earl. How strange. He must have left before sun-up.

Odd he hadn't stayed to say goodbye.

But she was grateful for his help the day before and hoped he would make it safe wherever he was going. She was proud of her hunting success and knew it was thanks to him. She gave silent thanks as she finished her breakfast and prepared for the ride home.

The descent from the woods was slow, taking most of the day. Ray let Rain pick his way down the trail and through the difficult rocky ground. The sun was bright in the sky, so she kept her hat dipped low to shield her eyes. Ray became hypnotised by the steady rhythm of Rain's hooves and the constant weight of the sun on her head. There wasn't a cloud in the sky and the air was still and silent, as if the earth was waiting. Waiting, and holding its breath. Step by step, they made their way across the hard baked ground, until eventually, late in the day, the homestead came into view.

Ray felt her heart lift at the sight of home, and she urged Rain to a trot, keen to feel the cool shadow of the barn and the safety of her cabin. Distance was deceptive in the haze of the sun. Her shadow was stretching long by the time she'd reached the safety of home. Rain picked up the pace when they got closer, raising his head and sniffing the air as if he could smell his stall.

Ray dismounted and untied her kill from Rain's saddle, throwing the carcasses onto the veranda. She was conscious she needed to prepare the meat as soon as possible, so it didn't go off. But first, she knew she had to see to Rain. He was tired and thirsty from the long ride back. Ray smiled at the cool air of evening and the familiar smell of the barn, the musky scent of horse, leather and oats, sweet and comforting.

Where was Rio?

She'd expected to see his nose over the gate welcoming her, but the stall appeared empty. She approached, curious, rather than worried, catching a reassuring glimpse of him. She was so pleased to re-unite with her best friend. She drew closer.

But he was lying down.

This wasn't right. She let go of Rain and ducked under the bar to check on Rio. He was still. Not a movement. A feeling of dread gripped her. Panicking, she threw herself forward. Kneeling by his side, she touched him, caressed him. But his body was cold, his eyes dull and lifeless; there were flecks of white round his mouth.

Ray screamed. A noise full of pain and anguish.

Not Rio, not her baby.

She lay her head on his cold flank, gripping him tightly as her body heaved and tears flowed until she was blinded by them. Her world spun, until she had no option but to crawl to the side of the barn and vomit.

'Rio,' she cried, 'Rio. Rio.'

She wiped her mouth with her sleeve and crawled back to the body of her pony, her best friend. She lay down next to him, her arm across his neck, breathing in his familiar scent. There she stayed, motionless as her horse, whilst night blanketed the barn in darkness.

When she woke it was still dark, but she sensed dawn wasn't far away. For an instant, Ray allowed herself to hope she'd fallen asleep with exhaustion and had a nightmare. But Rio's body still lay there, lifeless. She felt a cold hand gripping her heart and panic churning her insides. Layers of pain, like waves of broken glass, smashing against her heart. Her head still span with the impossibility of it. Thoughts burst like pinpricks behind her eyes.

How did he die? Why did he die? What killed him? What would she do now?

Suddenly, the air in the barn felt oppressive and rank. She needed to get out into the open. Ray crawled out under the bar toward the barn doors. Rain was standing, still with his saddle and bridle on, saddle bags slung across his back. She felt a pang of guilt. He'd served her well over the past few days and she had neglected him. Ray stripped off his tack and quickly brushed him down. She grabbed a bucket and filled it with water holding it under Rain's head, so he could drink.

'Steady there boy' she said, gently, 'not too much straight away or you'll get sick too.'

She let him drink a little more and then coaxed him into the stall next to Rio's. She needed to give him oats after the previous days' exertions. That was when she noticed the bucket of oats on the floor, in Rio's stall. A thought hit her like a hammer blow to the head.

Had she left the bucket of oats there?

She couldn't remember giving Rio any oats before she'd left. Why would she? He wasn't doing any work. She was sure she'd just left him with some chaff and water.

Little by little thoughts formed into a chain — someone had given Rio the oats — the oats were bad, poisoned — someone had murdered her precious Rio. Fierce, wild anger erupted inside her. It expanded from her heart to fill the very extremities of her body — hard and sharp, it tore at her insides. Fury built inside her until she could bear it no more. She vomited again, but the anger wasn't purged. Her knees buckled and she collapsed to the floor clutching her belly. She felt herself wrenched from her body, floating upwards she saw herself curled and writhing on the floor. She drifted higher and higher. And the higher she floated the more the pain dissipated. She could breathe again. She felt wings unfurl from her back. And on she flew, higher still. She could see the landscape below, moving from dry plains to lush rich forest. Homesteads and ranches dotting the landscape, people and creatures no bigger than grains of sand. She allowed the gentle wind to support her, until exhaustion overtook her wings.

Ray was awoken by a hand on her shoulder. She opened her eyes to look directly into black shining eyes.

Earl?

Reality crashed back and she felt the sharp burst of pain as she remembered Rio lying dead in the stall. She opened her mouth to tell Earl, but he placed a finger over her lips.

'It's ok Ray. I know. I've seen him. He's gone. But you're not. We need to get you cleaned up and then we can sort this mess out.'

Earl helped Ray stand. She felt weak, but the feelings of lonesome panic had curiously receded. Earl helped her outside and across the yard to the cabin. He took a seat on the veranda, whilst Ray went inside to clean herself. She emerged sometime later with fresh coffee. Earl was sitting patiently waiting.

'How did you find me?' she asked. 'My place is nearly a day's ride from where we camped. And where did you go, you weren't there when I woke up?'

Earl held up a hand to stop her flood of questions, letting out a soft laugh.

'Ray, truth be told, I'm a travelling man. Means I travel, and when I travel, I find places, and people, and things — that's all. And now it seems I found you.'

Ray suddenly remembered the oats. She slammed her cup down, coffee sloshing over the lip.

'The oats!' she yelled, running to the barn. As she burst through the doors, a startled Rain watched her ducking under the bar into Rio's stall. The pain of loss was burning again, as she saw Rio's lifeless body. She tore her eyes from him, grabbing the bucket of oats, she carried it out into the sunlight. Earl watched, as she dumped the bucket on the ground. Ray looked up at him.

'He was poisoned. I don't remember giving him oats when I left, but that bucket was in his stall. That means someone gave him the oats and that someone murdered him.'

Earl took a breath. His gaze dropped from Ray to the bucket.

'Well, that's possible, I guess,' he said slowly. 'But maybe you forgot that you gave him oats? Maybe those oats were bad, if the rats had got to them. You can't be sure that someone did this is all I'm saying.'

Ray felt anger erupting again. Her voice rose, as she spoke the thoughts that she'd suppressed up to now.

'I bet it's that Dwain Mickleton, son of a bitch. He'll do anything to get me off this land.' As she spoke the words, Ray felt them come true. Tears started to fall and she glared at Earl.

'Swear to God, I'll make him pay'.

Nine

5 years ago:

It was always when Ma and Pa were in town, or away doing work for others, that Pete made his regular visits to the homestead. Whenever she was home alone, Ray had taken to watching out for him. Anticipation, excitement, and disappointment when he didn't appear, were a constant mix of emotions that churned inside her, independent of conscious thought.

A smile would come unbidden when she recognised Pete's horse approaching, looking like it was floating on the billowing dust around its hooves. Pete's horse suited him. She was a roan mare with a long neck, her head hanging low as she loped along. The sun shone off her well-brushed haunches, shining speckled red. Pete's horse never looked like she was rushing anywhere, but she covered the ground as quick as any horse Ray had seen.

Pa had taken Ma to send herbs to another homesteader and Ray, as usual, stayed behind. Pete arrived as Ray was seeing to Rio after an early ride. Ray grabbed a couple of curry combs, and with an easy companionship, they stood each side of the horse combing off the dust and loose hair. Ray laughed as the horsehair carried on the breeze drifting through the barn doors. It floated aimlessly, highlighted by the fractured sunlight. Pete watched Ray as she followed it transfixed; her eyes alight with wonder.

She fascinated him. He spent many an hour out on the ranch thinking about her, when his mind should have been on his work. She looked different from anyone he'd ever met, with her wild hair and pale blue eyes. Folks in these parts didn't like different, fearful of what they didn't understand. Ray's appearance and her demeanour made people nervous. Some folks thought she was simple, and others said she was a child of the devil, making the sign of the cross when they saw her. But Pete didn't think much to any of that. He saw a strangely beautiful girl with a mind that didn't operate like anyone else. She saw beauty in things others didn't. She could watch the dust motes in the air, joy in her sparkling eyes, transported to another world that no-one else knew. Ray spoke the words in her head straight as they came, or she didn't speak at all. Pete didn't think she was frightening or dangerous, he thought she was fragile and special, and he wanted to be around her. Ray's voice broke into his thoughts.

'What are you doing there Pete, daydreaming when we've still got work to do.' She laughed, nudging at him with her elbow as she walked past. 'We need to saddle soap this tack or the leather's going to dry out and crack.'

Ray tossed her curry comb to one side and, reaching into a bucket, she pulled out a block of saddle soap and some cloths. She dunked them into water and wrung them out on the floor of the barn, but before she could start cleaning the saddle, they were interrupted by Lena's appearance in the doorway of the barn. Ray looked up, smiling at her Ma, calling out.

'Hey Ma.' Lena ignored Ray and focussed her attention on Pete.

'What're you doing here?'

Her words came clipped, through the hard set of her mouth.

'Howdy Ma'am.'

Pete took a step away from Rio.

'I was just passing nearby and thought I'd look in on Ray.'

He smiled politely, waiting for a response. When it came it was abrupt and unwelcoming.

'Well, I think it's time you headed off back to your own place Pete. Ray has chores to be getting on with. It ain't seemly for you to be out here with Ray when neither me nor her Pa's about.'

Pete nodded, picking his hat off a stall post and putting it on. He smiled politely at Lena. After casting a quick glance at Ray, who was already starting to soap up the saddle, he headed to the door. As he got level with Lena, he turned.

'I'll be seeing you, Ray,' he said.

Ray waved in Pete's direction, but didn't answer; her attention was fixed on the saddle she was cleaning. Lena stood in the doorway watching as Pete mounted his horse and rode off without a backwards glance. She watched till he was a speck in the distance.

Then she headed back to the cabin.

Several weeks later Ma announced a family visit to town. She insisted Ray be clean and presentable for the trip, ordering her to change into her clean spare skirt — the one covered with so many patches it was hard to make out the original fabric.

Ray filled a jug and bowl and washed herself in the barn. She'd rinsed her thick tresses the day before letting the sun and wind dry them as she worked. With her now clean shining locks and her over-patched skirt, Ray climbed into the wagon, settling in for the bumpy ride.

She was nervous about visiting town. She didn't go there often, but she and Ma needed new skirts. As she'd grown taller than Ma, her skirt had to be fitted, rather than rely on Ma choosing one from the rack. Then there were supplies to be brought, whilst they had the money. Pa had managed to get some extra work building fences for a ranch two day's ride hence. He'd been away for over a week and came home smiling with a pocket full of coin. Ma was keen to get the money spent on things they needed before Pa was tempted to chance his luck at the poker table. Ray suffered the bumping and jolting of the wagon with agitated anticipation. Town both scared and excited her. The ladies in their fine dresses, the thumping and clatter of horses and carts down Main Street, and the chatter of the town folk assaulted her senses. She was so used to the quiet of the homestead, town was a place of trepidation.

As the cart bumped its way down Main Street Ma and Pa discussed what they would get done in town. Pa needed shells for the rifle, saddle soap, and feed for the horses. Ma wanted skirts and foodstuffs from the grocer. Ray frowned, hearing Pa sharply telling Ma to keep Ray with her. Not to let her wander around talking to strangers. She shrugged, letting their fretful words drift over her, distracted by the novel sights and sounds. Before she knew it, Pa was pulling the wagon up to a hitching post. He jumped down and secured the reins. Then he headed off down the street without even a word, or a glance back in their direction. Ma was left to climb down from buckboard unaided. Ray needed no assistance to scramble off the back. With a determined look on her face, Ma walked calmly down the street toward the clothing store, her steps sure and steady. As they reached the shop two well-dressed women, walking arm in arm, were coming out. The younger had her nose in the air; laughter, false as a cracked bell, came out of her pouty mouth.

As they approached, Ma smiled at them, fixing her gaze on the older of the two.

'How do, Mary? I hope all's well with you, and Anna.'

She gave a small smile in the direction of the younger. Ray watched, as Anna's laughter dried up, her face reddening. She avoided both Ma and Ray's gaze and clutched her mother's arm a little tighter. Mary stiffened, looking directly at Lena.

'How do, Lena? We're very well thank you. I hope the same goes for you.'

Her words might be friendly, but her tone was leaden. This paradox confused Ray. Mary knew Ma, but the tension between them didn't speak of friendship.

Ray attempted a smile.

'How do,' she said softly, unsure how to make her words sound. The women ignored her like she wasn't there. Mary gave a final nod to Ma, before she and Anna hurried away.

Ray looked at Ma, questioningly. She didn't understand what had occurred. Ma remained silent, her expression unreadable, and led her inside. Once they were in the store, Ma chose two skirts, one for her, one for Ray. They were plain and cheap and other than ensuring the right fit for Ray, they didn't take much choosing. They left the store not more than ten minutes after they'd entered. As they walked down the street, Ray asked Ma:

'Who were those women Ma. How do you know them?'

'I know lots of women round these parts, most not so well. Sometimes they need my help with birthing, and such like, with the herbs.' Ma gave a slight shrug before adding, 'Don't mean they like it though.'

Ray wasn't sure what Ma meant by those words. But she let them slide past without further thought, turning her attention to the world around her. Not a second or two later, they came level with the saloon. The doors opened, and they heard the muffled sounds of laughter and the chatter of men. Pa came out, pulling up short when he saw Ma and Ray. Ma stopped and glared at him, hands on hips.

'What are you looking at woman?' Pa spat the words. 'Ain't a man allowed to have a whiskey with the money he earned by hard work and sweat.'

Ma answered sharp and brittle.

'Two minutes we been in town, and you head straight to the saloon when my back's turned. Sure hope your poke ain't empty.'

'God Damit woman stop your nagging, I had me a whiskey or two while doing some business. That's man's business you understand, not yours.'

Ray watched Pa's face darken. Whiskey made Pa quick to anger and she knew how fast quiet words turned loud and angry when Ma and Pa had at it. But before either of them could speak again, the saloon door opened, and two more men exited. The first man through the door was tall and barrel chested, his dark eyebrows thick and heavy, casting a shadow over his features. His eyes slid over Pa and came to rest on Ma, his gaze narrowing and his lips forming a thin sharp line. He tipped his hat.

'Lena,' he said, just that.

When Ma responded her tone was neither friendly nor hostile.

'Jared, it's been a long time. How's Sally doing these days?'

'Sally's fine, thank you for asking.'

The man spoke mechanically, and quickly, as if he wanted to get the words out and move on. Before he could, Pa grabbed his arm and pulled him to the side. As he did so, Ray saw the second man in the doorway, and as he stepped forward, she recognised Pete. Seeing her, his face broke into a smile. He edged past the two men, trotting down the steps to her. He smiled a greeting to Ma. But Ma's attention was on Pa and Jared.

'It sure is good to see you Ray, I've missed you these past couple of weeks.'

Ray smiled back at Pete and her heart flipped a little in her chest. Before she could respond, Pete was speaking again.

'We've sure been busy out on the ranch these last weeks with calving season. The herd's growing nicely now. One of these days, it'll be too big for us, but for now it's keeping us pretty busy.'

'I'd sure like to see one of those calves,' Ray blurted. 'I bet they're real pretty.'

Her hands clutched her skirt. One foot tapped anxiously on the dirt road.

Pete laughed.

'I guess you could say they're pretty when they're real little, but they get big mighty quick. Maybe one day I'll come get you and you can lend us a hand. You have a way with the horses, so maybe you can tame them cattle too.'

Ray smiled shyly, she liked the idea of spending time with Pete and helping with the newborn calves. But her thoughts were interrupted by the barrel-chested man. His words were blunt edged and hard.

'Pete!' he shouted, 'there ain't no time for you to be standing around talking. Get the horses, we need to be heading back to the ranch.'

'Yes Pa.'

Pete gave Ray a final smile before striding off in the direction of their horses. Ray looked up to see Jared Mickleton glaring at her, as he rammed his Stetson on his head and started off after his son.

Ray didn't know why he seemed so angry. She turned to Ma, but she didn't recognise the look on her face. She seemed preoccupied and sad, something about her expression was unfathomable. Ray didn't have the words to ask why. She looked up again to find Pa no longer there. Ma took her arm and led her away. Her touch was gentle and her voice soft when she spoke.

'Come along girl, let's get the rest of what we need, then we can head on back home.'

Ten

Ray walked purposefully toward the barn, anger simmering beneath the surface, bubbling in the pit of her stomach. Her anger made her feel strong and powerful. She felt herself expanding and solidifying, strength radiating from her. She could take on anyone and anything, and today she would take on Dwain Mickleton. When Ray reached the barn, she grabbed Rain's saddle from where she'd left it on the floor. Avoiding looking at the rigid body of Rio in his stall, she saddled up. The bags and gear from her hunting trip were still on the barn floor. She grabbed the Winchester rifle and rammed her Colt pistol into the holster at her waist. Leading Rain out of the barn, she found Earl standing in front of the doors. His body cast a long shadow, like a dark river, across the entrance to the barn. He looked intently at Ray and spoke slowly and calmly.

'Ray, I'm not sure this is the best course of action. You going over to the Mickleton ranch carrying this much anger.'

'They killed my horse.' Ray said, the tremor in her voice reflecting the emotions coursing through her.

'You *think* they killed your horse,' answered Earl. 'You said yourself; you can't be sure. You go in there half-cocked, and someone is likely to get killed, and that someone is just as likely to be you.'

Ray silently mounted Rain. Her head high, her back rigid.

'I'm going, no matter what you say. I can go by myself, or you can come with me. It's your choice.'

Earl walked slowly toward Ray and offered her his arm. Ray grabbed it and Earl swung himself up behind her. Without a word, Ray kicked Rain into a trot, and they headed toward the Mickleton ranch.

As they reached the ranch, Ray let out a rough laugh. The Mickleton's had set up a wooden gate at the entrance to their land with their name carved across the top.

'Look at these people,' spat Ray, dark humour colouring her voice. 'They're just regular folk like the rest of us homesteaders. They got a few cattle is all and they call it a ranch. You'd think they was something special putting their name up at the door, better than the rest of us.'

Ray reined her horse to a halt in front of the gates.

'Dwain Mickleton,' she shouted, 'you son of a bitch, where the fuck are you?' Her voice echoed out loud and strong in the air, breaking the silence.

'You come out here right now or I'm coming in for you.'

A hollow silence fell as Ray waited. She wondered if she was going to have to ride in. Then she caught movement by the doors to the barn. Two men she didn't recognise walked out. Cowboys moving like they lived their lives on horseback, spurs tinkling in time with their footsteps. Both men were armed with revolvers holstered on their hips. One of them held a rifle in the crook of his arm, pointing down at the ground.

They came to a stop some fifty paces from Ray.

'What do you want, lady?' called the man carrying the rifle, his voice rough and his tone impatient. 'State your business.'

'I want Dwain Mickleton,' shouted Ray, anger carrying her voice.

'Well lady, the boss ain't expecting you, and he's mighty busy today, so best you ride on back to where you came from.'

Neither he, nor the other cowboy, seemed bothered by Ray's presence. She was no threat, just a bothersome interruption.

Ray's hand moved menacingly towards her Colt.

'You better get him out here or I'll be coming in for him.'

'That won't be necessary,' came a deep voice from the barn doorway.

Ray turned to see Dwain and Pete coming out of the barn. Dwain wore two revolvers on his belt and Pete cradled a rifle in his arms.

The brothers continued pacing forwards until they were flanking the cowboys. Four of them standing in an arc looking directly at Ray. She remained seated on her horse. Anger, strength, fear, righteousness, all mixed up in her mind.

'Why d'you kill my horse?' she yelled, emotion straining her voice.

'What you talking about?' drawled Dwain, disdainfully, 'I think you might be a little crazy lady.'

Ray's anger came to boiling point.

How dare he act like she was the problem, calling her crazy for saying the truth.

'You killed my horse!' she shouted, anger feeding the pitch of her voice. She felt herself shaking as tears pricked at the corners of her eyes. 'You poisoned his oats, and you killed him while I was away hunting.'

Dwain's face hardened and when he spoke his voice was rough, like the sound of the gravel underfoot.

'Now lady, you should be real careful before you go around accusing people of killing horses. You better have proof of that, is all I'm saying, 'cos a man would be within his rights to defend himself against accusations like that.'

Ray felt the air solidify, as the men's eyes bored into her. They seemed to tense. She saw the cowboy with the rifle slowly raise the barrel towards her. As he spoke, Dwain's hand slipped down from his belt until his fingers grazed the handle of his revolver.

'Now I suggest Ray, you turn that mount of yours around and ride back out of here. If you want to accuse me of killing your horse, take that to the Sheriff, and you better have some goddam proof.'

Ray felt the grip of the Colt under her fingertips; she yearned to yank it from the holster. But fear and uncertainty began pricking at her edges. She wasn't sure what her next move should be.

'You killed my horse 'cos you want my land,' she blurted, her words now more appeal than challenge.

Dwain stepped forward; anger palpable. Words controlled and even.

'Lady, I will take your land 'cos you're not fit to have it, and you owe me. But I'll take it by the law, or I'll take it when you're gone. You're going to kill yourself out there by yourself, I don't have to do nothing to you, you're going to do it all to yourself. Now, for the last time, get the hell off my land.'

Ray glared at Dwain. The men around him fanned outwards, the cowboy's rifle trained on her. Dwain's hand twitched over his pistol, just waiting for her to make a move. She glanced at Pete. His rifle still pointed at the ground; his eyes downcast. She felt Earl's breath on her neck. Words floated softly into her ear.

'This can't end well; you're outnumbered and outgunned — time to head back.'

Ray's eyes lingered on the men for a few more seconds then she turned Rain around and kicked him to a canter.

Ray untacked Rain and led him into his stall. She was still trembling with the confusion of emotions. Sadness weighed heavy on her, its edges tainted by anger and fear. She felt helpless. The Mickleton's and their men had made her feel powerless. Even carried by the strength of her anger, they had made her fearful and she was the weaker for it. She glanced at Rio's body in the stall, cold and rigid. It wouldn't be long before the body would stink. She needed to do something with him. She felt at a loss. Turning she caught Earl standing behind, staring at her with compassion in his eyes.

'We need to do something about the body,' he said, like he'd read her mind. 'It's going to putrefy and that's dangerous. Best we should burn it.'

Ray shook her head. No, she couldn't do that to Rio. The thought of him burning made her sick to her stomach.

'No Earl, I can't do that.'

She thought for a moment.

'I'm going to go into town. Going to tell the Sheriff about it, just like Dwain said. Maybe I can get someone to come out and take the body. That's what I'll do. Ain't no time to do it now; I'll do it in the morning.'

Next day Ray harnessed Rain to the wagon and drove into town. She'd not been able to feed him any oats, as she didn't know whether the whole sack had been poisoned. She'd have to buy some more in town, and more rifle shells. But her first stop would be the Sheriff. Ray jumped down from the wagon and tied Rain to the rail outside the Sheriff's office. She found him with his feet on his desk, drinking coffee.

His smile came slowly.

'Good morning there Ray,' he said, squinting at her.

She'd lost weight; men's pants hung loose accentuating her tall, spare frame. After weeks without brushing, her hair was even more voluminous. Thick red ropes forced their way from under her hat to tumble over her shoulders and down her back. Her pale skin was darkened by a film of dirt. Her blue eyes framed by sun-bleached eyelashes, shone bright despite the dullness threatening to envelop her. The Sheriff felt a wave of pity for this strange and exotic creature.

Standing, he gestured to a chair.

'Take a seat there, Ray,' he said softly.

As she sat, he poured a mug of coffee, handing it to her before returning to his chair. 'Now what can I do for you?'

Ray took a deep breath and explained what had happened to Rio. She felt sadness threatening to overwhelm her, but she tried to keep her voice level and clear. She spoke what she knew to be the truth. All the time she held the image of Rio's body in the stall and felt the weight of her grief. When she finished talking, the Sheriff rose from his chair and began pacing the room. He lifted his hat and scratched his head, before turning and looking at Ray.

'Accusing someone of killing your horse on your land is pretty serious, Ray. I understand there's bad blood between you and the Mickletons, but do you have any evidence that it was Dwain that did this?' He scratched his head again before resuming his pacing.

'Horses die sometimes, Ray. They get ill, they get bitten by snakes. The oats could have gone bad, 'specially if the rats had got to them. Why, there's all sorts of reasons why your horse might have died that don't have nothing to do with Dwain.'

Ray sat silently. She saw pity in the Sheriff's eyes. He spoke kindly, but he pitied her, and it was clear that he didn't believe her. Ray got up from her chair. She couldn't conceal her anger as she made to leave. The Sheriff flapped his hand, gesturing for her to sit.

'Look Ray, I don't want you to go away from here with thoughts of revenge in your mind. You don't want to be making things any worse for yourself.'

Ray shook her head in frustration.

'What do you expect me to do, Sheriff? They killed my horse, and they're trying to take my land.'

She looked around her, wishing that she'd brought Earl. She needed his calm influence. He'd know what to say to the Sheriff.

The Sheriff paused his pacing and looked down at Ray.

'Listen Ray, I think it's highly unlikely Dwain Mickleton would poison your horse. It's not his style to be sneaking around like that.

Quite frankly, I'd believe you more if you said he'd got angry and shot the horse.'

The Sheriff paused again; Ray could see a thought sliding across his face. 'Ray, did you bring any of the oats with you, the ones in the bucket?'

Ray shook her head. She felt foolish now. Of course, she should have brought the oats. Before she could speak, the Sheriff continued.

'What I'm going to do Ray is send a deputy over to your place to collect some of the oats and then we'll look to find some poor creature to test them on. At least that way we'll know if the oats are bad. If one of my boys is out there, he can stop in and have a word with the Mickletons, whilst he's about it.'

Ray went to speak, but the Sheriff carried on.

'And even if they are bad, that still don't mean that your horse was poisoned on purpose. Those oats might just have gone bad, but it might give us some clarity as to the situation.'

Ray smiled her thanks at the Sheriff and turned to leave. She wasn't sure what she had expected the Sheriff to do — head straight out to the Mickleton's and arrest Dwain? No, this was the best she could expect given the circumstances. She'd just have to wait and see how things played out.

Eleven

Smoke!

There was smoke, billowing clouds of it coming right from her homestead. Ray's eyes widened and panic flooded through her.

Oh God, no, not my home!

Dense black smoke met the haze from the sun and cast strange shapes in the air. This swirling wall blinded her as she urged Rain to pull the wagon faster. Closer, an overwhelming sense of dread engulfed her. An acrid stench of burning assaulted her nostrils. Gritty smoke stung her eyes, sending tears cascading down her cheeks.

Come on, Rain. Come on!

Abruptly she emerged through the choking barrier and there was her homestead.

It was safe.

Her cabin and barn stood solid and secure behind a burning pyre. She pulled on the reins, slowing the wagon. Her urge to rush forward conflicted with the need to hang back and take stock of the situation. There were men around the fire, faces covered with bandanas, working with shovels to keep the flames contained.

What the hell?

Who were they? What were they doing on her land? What were they burning? As she got closer one of the men walked toward her. He pulled his bandana down and stood, waiting for her.

Pete?

Ray knew Pete. She trusted Pete. He had been there for her since Ma and Pa died, helping her when he could. But this? This wasn't right. Ray pulled Rain to a halt and jumped off the cart, rushing forward, panic and confusion giving her voice a shrillness she didn't recognise.

'What the hell are you doing? What the fuck are you doing on my land?'

Pete intercepted Ray as she rushed for the fire.

'Hold up there girl. It's OK, it's OK.'

Pete grabbed at Ray's arm as she tried to rush past him, her eyes fixed on the fire. 'Calm down,' he urged, pulling her back. 'Please Ray, just wait, listen to me.'

Ray felt Pete's grip on her arm. Firm, strong, comforting, but restricting. She pulled, trying to jerk her arm free, but felt her strength ebbing. She allowed Pete to stop her. Still holding her arm, he moved to stand between her and the fire, his eyes imploring.

'Listen to me Ray, just listen. I brought a couple of the boys from the ranch over to take care of your pony. I know how you felt about him, like he was more than just a horse, like he was a part of you. I knew you couldn't do what needed to be done and that's why I came. To do it for you. When you weren't here it seemed like it was meant to be. That I could sort it out for you, so you didn't have to. I wanted to do it for you Ray.'

Ray stood, rigid, fixed to the spot. Pete's words slowly sinking in. She looked from Pete and then to the fire, and back again.

'Rio?'

'That's right Ray, we had to burn him. Ain't safe to have him lying around, not if there's poison in him. Besides in this heat the body's just going to rot and you don't want that.'

Ray gasped, she couldn't take it in, she couldn't breathe. Her head spun, knees buckling, blackness creeping into the corners of her eyes. It was too much. She felt her legs go, but Pete was there, he caught her, his hands under her shoulders, supporting her. She felt his closeness and for a second allowed herself to be held by him. But then, with a rush of fresh strength, she broke away, brushing off his hands, stepping back. Her gaze drifted between Pete and the fire. His eyes soft as sky contrasted with the hellish flames licking off the remains of her Rio.

'Please Ray,' implored Pete. 'Please, come sit down, just for a minute.'

Ray followed Pete to the veranda. The air was clearer, the wind blew the flames and the smoke away from the cabin. Pete handed her a small flask of whiskey.

'Here Ray, have a drink.'

After a few slugs Ray slumped back in a chair. This was too much for her to take in. She directed her thoughts away from Rio, attempting to absorb Pete's words.

'I'm sorry, really I am,' said Pete, 'Maybe I should have waited for you. Talked to you first. But I was just trying to help. The body would have gone bad, and other critters could have eaten those oats, spreading the poison. You know it had to be done.'

Slowly his words penetrated. Tendrils of meaning spread through her. She looked at the fire; and then something hit her.

The oats.

'You burned the oats?' she yelled, jumping up and running down the steps toward the fire. Pete leapt up; grabbing Ray's arm he swept her from the flames.

'Jesus girl! Get back! You'll get burned.'

Ray stared at the fire, flames dancing before her eyes. There was nothing there anymore. Everything was gone. Her anger dissipated as quickly as it had risen. She felt hollow as she gazed up at the blue sky and the coils of smoke floating on the breeze. She didn't want to be here. She was sick and tired of the emotions flooding her body and mind — anger, frustration, misery.

'What have you done Pete? I needed those oats. I told the Sheriff your brother poisoned them. He said he'd test them to see if that was true. Why did you burn them Pete? Did Dwain tell you to do it?'

Pete took a step back from Ray.

'You did what? You told the Sheriff that Dwain poisoned your horse? Dammit Ray! It ain't enough you came out to the ranch and accused my brother of using poison, you had to tell the Sheriff.'

Pete snatched the bandana from his neck, wiping off dirt and tears newly brimming his eyes.

'For God's sake Ray. I know bad luck's been following you around lately, but don't mean you got to act crazy. Coming out to our place and shooting your mouth off to Dwain like you did is liable to get you nothing but a bullet. You're chasing things that ain't there.'

Pete sighed. Soon the pyre would burn itself out. He stared at Ray. He truly wanted to help her. But she needed to start helping herself too — beginning by making smart choices. He willed himself to speak calmly.

'These are bad times girl. I wish they was different. I wish your Ma and Pa weren't dead. I wish your pony weren't dead. Hell, I wish we had some rain. Lots of things I done wish for but life ain't as clean as that. Those oats of yours probably just went bad, I don't know. Hell, might not even been the oats that killed him. But what I do know is you need to start focusing on surviving, not chasing ghosts, and not looking to blame others for your troubles.'

Ray twisted around to face him.

'Your brother wants my land,' she said, cold and flat.

'Ray, listen to me. Your Pa owed a debt to mine and now they're dead that debt sits between you and Dwain. Yeah, sure, he wants some of your land; he ain't made no secret of that. Him and Melvin been talking about it for months before they died.'

Pete's words drifted over her, loose in the air. She remembered when Pa was here, and Ma, and Rio. Life felt like it would carry on forever, life ebbing and flowing season by season. But now, she was adrift, alone. She tried to take in Pete's words.

'With this drought we ain't got enough grazing for our cattle, and your place is not much good to anyone with your corn dying. Seems foolish to me to let two places go to hell. Anyhow, Dwain, well he may be a hard man, but he's stand-up. He wouldn't stoop so low as to poison a pony. He's just sitting by, waiting, 'cos if you carry on like you are, you're just going to kill yourself out here, and he'll claim the land when you're dead. Sheriff says...'

'Sheriff says what?' jumped in Ray. 'You mean you've been talking to the Sheriff about taking my land, about me?'

'There's a debt Ray. It ain't your fault it's there, but that don't mean it can go away just 'cos you want it to. There's got to be a way to make so as everyone's OK. I know there is.'

Ray stood in silence. A jumble of thoughts filled her head. Indistinct, fragmented thoughts she couldn't put to words. Right now, she wanted desperately to be alone. She wanted to be free. Her gaze turned toward the glowing embers. Up to now she'd only seen flames, but now she saw her pony, her friend. She saw his spirit lick up into the sky, like he was galloping free. Tears tumbled down her dirty face, leaving jagged pale tracks.

'Rio,' she said quietly to herself. Pete stepped forward placing his heavy hand gently on her shoulder.

'Say a prayer if'n you want,' he whispered.

'Don't know no prayers.'

'Then think of him and the good times, hold his memory and

say goodbye.'

They watched as the embers dimmed; eventually there was nothing but ashes. Ray wiped the tears from her eyes as she wordlessly bid farewell to her Rio, feeling another tiny piece of her heart break.

Pete sensed the moment. It was time for him to leave. Time for Ray to be alone with her thoughts.

Ray woke with the sun low in the sky and a chill creeping through the air. She was still in the chair on the veranda. Her body felt cold and stiff. It was hard to open her eyes. Some part of her wanted to sleep and never wake up. She felt a gentle hand laid on top of hers, pulling her forward, pulling her awake. She willed herself from her slumbers. Above her was Earl's face, his deep brown eyes offering her comfort.

'You're awake now, that's good. It's getting pretty cold out here Ray, you need to come in and light the fire, have some food, and try and get some sleep.'

He waited whilst she levered herself out of the chair, her limbs stiff and awkward. Once inside, Ray set about lighting a fire. The cold had set into her bones, and she felt herself shiver deep inside. She put a pot on the fire with some meat to boil and some corn from last year. The corn was nearly finished, and it wouldn't be long before she'd have to harvest what remained of the stunted cobs growing in the field out back. As her food cooked, and her coffee brewed, Ray turned to Earl.

'Why did you let them come in here and do that?' she spoke quietly. 'You just let them burn my horse and the oats. Why didn't you stop them?'

Earl returned her pleading look with one of sympathy.

'What can I do against Pete Mickleton and his cowboys? Nothing is what. Besides I wasn't here. I took a walk. But I'm here now and I'm going to take care of you.'

Ray let out a sigh, turning her attention to pouring herself coffee. She felt stuck, like a jack rabbit caught in a snare. She didn't have enough money to buy food and supplies to last the winter, and her crops were failing in the drought. She needed rain and lots of it. She needed a miracle.

Twelve

The air in the ranch house was hot and oppressive, thickened by the aroma of simmering meat. Dwain and Pete sat at the rough-hewn table whilst Ma set about the kitchen, preparing their meal. Both men sat in silence. They looked younger without the trappings of adult masculinity — holsters and hats, and the grime of the working day. They'd washed the dirt from their faces, and wet down their hair, slicking it to their heads. Sitting at the table patiently waiting for their meal, they looked like the children they had once been. At twenty-five, Dwain was the oldest. He resembled their Pa. Dark hair and broad features were set rigid on his face, telling of a hard life of work and the weight of responsibility. Pete was taller and slimmer, his features smaller and his hair lighter, making him look younger than his twenty-two years.

Sally Mickleton was at the stove with her back to them, fussing with a stew pot. She was tall, moving with a stateliness of bearing. Her shoulders were square and her back straight. She appeared unbowed by the hard life of a ranch wife — now widow. Her grey hair was gathered in a tight bun; the skin of her neck was yet unwrinkled and smooth. At a glance you'd think she was younger than her forty-five years. But her dull eyes and lined features betrayed her true age.

'You look pale, Ma,' said Dwain with concern. 'You should spend a little time in the sun.'

'I might go sit on the veranda tomorrow son,' she replied, 'but you know I don't care much for being outside.'

Dwain and Pete exchanged a look. Dwain couldn't remember the last time Ma had ventured any further than the veranda. He knew that when she was young, she used to go out, to town, to church. Hell, that's how she'd met his Pa. But it had been years since she'd been any further than the picket fence at the edge of the veranda. Even as a small boy, he couldn't remember his Ma leaving the ranch. Now his Pa was dead, he and Pete were her only link with the world. Being the oldest, it was his responsibility to look after Ma and the ranch. He was going to do whatever it took to accomplish that — like his Pa did when he was alive.

Pete looked to his brother.

'I done took a couple of the boys out to Ray Crow's place today and burned her horse, and those damned oats,' he said quietly.

'I know.' said Dwain, gaze fixed ahead, voice expressionless.

Ma stirred the stew taking in their conversation.

Then Pete said, 'She went'n told the Sheriff you poisoned the oats and killed her horse.'

Dwain shook his head. When he spoke annoyance crept into his voice.

'Don't know where she'd get that idea. Woman's as crazy as a box of snakes and that's a bottom fact.'

'I burned the oats,' repeated Pete. 'Don't want them laying around if they're bad. Don't you reckon Dwain?'

'Reckon that's about right,' Dwain responded, before turning to look at his brother, his eyes had narrowed, and his forehead creased; irritation was mounting.

'An' I ain't real happy with your tone about now. You accusing me too?'

Pete lowered his gaze before answering.

'I'm just saying that it wouldn't be good to have bad oats lying around is all.'

Sally brought an end to the conversation.

'Dinner's ready you two.'

She ladled up bowls of stew and joined her sons sitting at the table. They ate in silence for a time before Sally spoke.

'Boys, I want to make something real clear. I never liked that Melvin Crow, and it weren't right he shot your Pa like that out in the street. And we could surely use some money, or extra land to keep this ranch going. That and some goddam rain. But...'

She paused, setting down her spoon, looking at Dwain and Pete in turn.

'I never had no beef with Lena Crow, in fact she done some real good for the women out in these parts, including me. I was mighty sad to hear about her passing, and I don't want no harm coming to her daughter by your hand, that clear?'

'Clear as a bell, Ma,' responded Pete.

Sally turned to her other son.

'Dwain?'

He raised his eyes from his bowl and looked his Ma square in the eye before responding.

'Sure Ma, clear as a bell.'

The rest of the meal was eaten in silence, save for the sound of good food being enjoyed. Once the meal was done, Sally sent the boys out onto the veranda with their coffee, whilst she set about washing and tidying up. Her hands moved as they ever did, when undertaking the tasks that constituted the building blocks of her existence. As she worked, her mind drifted into the past.

Lena Crow sat by the side of the bed and gently brushed a stray hair off Sally's forehead. As she did so, Sally opened her eyes. They looked at Lena with such a depth of sadness and despair that it took all of Lena's resolve to keep her features fixed in an expression of calmness and hope. Her face said everything would be alright. Everything will be fine. Except it wouldn't. Sally would most likely live through this, but she'd never be the same again. Lena knew that, for sure. She gently stroked Sally's forehead again, this time feeling the first beads of sweat appearing. She saw Sally's hands move to her stomach holding the gentle mound that was the source of her agony. She saw the mound contract, and a wave of pain passed over Sally's face. Sweat now drenched her forehead and top lip. She endured her suffering in silence. But Lena knew it wouldn't last. It never did.

'I'll be back in a second, Sally. Just hold on. I need to fetch some cool water and a cloth.' Lena quickly left the bedroom and headed outside to fetch a bucket of water. She saw that Jared had gotten the two boys in the wagon and was about to climb into the driving seat. When he saw Lena, he turned back toward her with a hard expression on his face, a scowl deepening the lines on his forehead.

'Will it be done when we get back?' he asked.

'One way or another,' Lena said.

She turned back toward the cabin hauling the water, without a backwards glance. She sighed heavily, hearing the steady clatter of hooves, and the rattling of the wagon, as Jared and the boys headed away to town.

Time Lena got back into the cabin, Sally had kicked the blanket off and had rolled onto her side. Her hands still clasped her belly and her face looked tight with pain, her lips pressed together into a hard line, and her skin so taught it looked like it might split open. Lena dipped a clean cloth into the cool water, and after wringing it out, she gently wiped the sweat from Sally's face.

'You got to try and breathe through the pain,' she whispered. 'I can't take the pain away, but it won't last forever, you just got to get through it while it's there.'

Sally writhed on the bed making fearful low groans. They sounded primal. Like they were coming from a place so deep they were impossible to contain. Tears wet her tight closed eyelids. Lena moved her gaze from Sally's face down her body and noticed the first tell-tale signs of blood between her legs. She gently moved Sally onto her back and watched as the blood pooled on the mattress. Sally's body began to jerk and spasm, small movements at first and then more violent.

'Sally, Sally!' yelled Lena, holding her down. 'Sally, are you with me? You need to force yourself to breathe deep and slow.'

Lena was frantic, her heart pounding. She couldn't lose Sally. She'd promised Jared she'd get Sally through this. Given her oath she'd be OK. Lena felt Sally's hot, sweat-damp forehead and whispered a prayer. A moment later Sally's body stilled. Lena lifted her eyelid; there was nothing but white. Lena collected a pan of hot water from the grate. Pushing up her sleeves she washed her hands.

Sally looked up at the cloudless sky and felt the warmth of the sun and the faint memory of the previous night's rain. The boys were napping in the back room, and with Jared in town, she had a moment's peace to get the washing done. She thanked God for her lot in life. This kind of living was hard. And with two young boys she was permanently exhausted. Yet still she was happy. She'd gotten what she'd always wanted: a husband, children, a place to call home.

Caught up in her own thoughts, Sally didn't hear the horses' hooves, as they approached. She didn't see the two men as they dismounted and walked toward her. She was startled when they spoke. Two men with eyes that shifted constantly and bodies that twitched. One was tall and lean, all limbs and bones. His skin so white he could be a ghost. He had the palest blue eyes she'd ever seen, whites bloodshot with whiskey. The other was stocky and grey, cheeks distorted by a wad of tobacco. They asked her where her man was.

'Out back,' she lied.

They laughed. The short man squirted tobacco juice onto the dirt.

'No lady, he ain't,' he said.

Sally willed herself not to look back at the cabin, to her boys, fast asleep dreaming childish dreams. The ghost man spoke, his voice deep and soft, making a lie of his appearance.

'We're on the bounty of Jim McLaugh, don't suppose you've seen him about? Maybe he passed through here?'

'No, we haven't seen anyone,' said Sally, attempting to calm her voice.

'Mmmm, well seeing as we're here, how about you make us a cup of coffee. It's a fair ride into town and we've been on the road since sun-up.'

Sally nodded and headed to the cabin. She had coffee warming on the stove. If she was quiet, she could serve the men without waking her boys.

'How 'bout you put some whiskey in that coffee. I expect your man keeps some,' said the ghost.

Sally came out of the cabin with two cups of coffee laced with whiskey. She handed a mug to each man and remained standing, trying not to watch them while they drank. They seemed edgy. Bounty hunters gone feral chasing their own kind. The morality of it all long forgotten. They stank of sweat, booze and violence. Sally knew how this would play out. She could see it in their shifting eyes and the way they looked at her. She couldn't run. Wouldn't run and desert her boys. Besides, where would she go? The men finished their coffee and walked toward her, stepping in awful unison. Sally looked up at the clear blue sky. Even so low, the sun blinded her, tears ran down her face.

Their hands were on her clothes. She willed herself to keep quiet, clenching her fists until her nails pierced her skin. She thought of her boys, blissfully unaware of what their mother was going through — their innocent faces soft with sleep. Then came the pain like an arrow piercing her. She couldn't hold back. Her mouth opened impossibly wide, and a scream erupted from deep inside.

Sally's eyes blinked open; she was in the ranch house. The sun was streaming through the window and the room was hot. She was stretched on her bed like a rag doll. The sheets were slick with blood and sweat. Through a haze of pain and tears, she could see Lena wrapping something in cloth. Once she'd finished, she looked up at Sally. With a sad smile, she shook her head slowly.

'It's done now Sally. I'll be back in a minute.'

As Lena left, Sally turned her head to the window and the blue sky beyond. Her lids drooped and she drifted away. When she awoke, she was still in bed, but the sheets were clean, and she was wearing a fresh nightdress. Lena was sat beside the bed once more watching her with the same sad smile on her face.

Thirteen

Ray woke with a start. Her dreams had been full of fire. Rio was a winged phoenix galloping through the flames. And she'd sat atop his back, her own wings spread behind her. Her limbs tingling with the heat of the fire; her heart beating fast; her breath coming in short fiery gasps.

She sat up in bed listening intently. What had dragged her from sleep? There were the usual noises the cabin made at night. The wood creaking gently as it shrunk with the cold, the crackle of the fire as it burned low, and the skittling and scuttling of insects and mice. There it was again, the sound that had awakened her, a *caaaw caaaw*, the cry piercing the night. As it's call faded, there was something else. A murmuring on the wind. Voices. Indistinct, but there, nevertheless. She strained her ears, but the voices were no more. After a while Ray thought maybe she was mistaken — tail end of a dream, maybe. There was nothing. No cause for alarm. But just as she'd settled back down, the murmurings started again. And this time they were accompanied by the sound of boots stealthily pacing the creaking planks of the veranda.

Ray's heart hammered in her chest; her lungs gulped in air. She forced herself to quieten her breathing, so she could concentrate on the noises outside. She looked around frantically. Her rifle was in the scabbard hanging off the back of the chair in the main room. Her Colt lay on the table. Throwing off her blankets she crept into the main room. She felt so vulnerable barefoot, wearing nothing but a pair of Pa's old long johns and a long-sleeved undershirt. The room was all moonlight shadows, with just a faint glimmer from the embers. She crept to the table, each step slow and careful, eyes fixed on the glinting steel of the Colt.

Was it even loaded?

The shells were in a box under her bed. Damn. As she neared the table the front door burst open, and two men charged into the cabin.

The first through the door saw Ray going for the revolver and rushed at her. They collided, sending the table crashing to the floor. Ray had the wind knocked out of her; pain exploded in her shoulder. She struggled to her knees. A gun smashed into her forehead. Gasping for air she flailed frantically, trying to rise. Her head caught the full force of a boot kick. Pain exploded in pin pricks of light, as she crashed back to the floor. Voices harsh and guttural, words inaudible. Another boot, this time in her belly, another smashing into her back. She howled with pain and shock.

Through the waves of agony she heard Earl's voice.

'Ray, Ray,' he said urgently, 'come on, come with me. Quick. Come quickly now.'

She felt him take her hand, pulling her gently. She felt herself rising from the hard unforgiving floor. She felt light and free — pain and confusion drifted away. Earl was leading her toward the smashed cabin door. She glanced back. The her of a moment ago was curled in a protective ball on the floor. Two men with twisted ugly faces were kicking her defenceless body. Before she could reason Earl tugged her hand. She blinked and they were out the door and running, running fast across the dust-dry plain. Her legs moved with speed and grace. A smile burst upon her face like the first light of a June morning. Her hand slipped from Earl's; she pumped her arms to drive herself forward faster. There were tingles in her back and a pleasurable aching itch. She looked down to find her feet no longer in contact with the earth. Glistening dark wings had sprouted and were propelling her skyward. She was effortlessly soaring, catching the warm updraft from the desert. The landscape moved rapidly around her, colours muted by the cool light of a full moon. And there was Earl alongside her, his wings flexing effortlessly in the thermals. Grinning at each other, they flew and flew until the first rays of the sun peeked over the horizon.

Ray relaxed her wings and allowed gravity to take her drifting gracefully to the ground. Her skin was tingling, and her face was set in a grin of the purest joy. She turned to Earl, so grateful for his presence. They watched the sun cresting the hills until its brightness became so fierce Ray had to close her eyes. Even then, she could see the ball of solar fire as clear as if her eyes were open.

She felt herself getting unbearably hot. Her joy rapidly reverting to pain.

When Ray dared open her eyes, she was back curled on the floor of the cabin, her breath rasping in her throat. The metallic taste of blood filled her mouth. Overwhelming pain lanced through her neck as she turned her head. To her astonishment Earl was kneeling next to her, his hand still holding hers. He stroked her forehead, whispering words of kindness. She screwed up her eyes in an attempt to clear her vision, to make sense of the devastation surrounding her.

Everything in the room was smashed and broken. The remains of her meal had been trampled by the intruders. She lay still and listened hard. After a while she concluded her attackers had long since gone. The bed was upended, the mattress slashed. Earl helped her onto her hands and knees. Every piece of her body screamed for her attention. Her lungs burned, her head throbbed, her limbs ached, and moving was all different kinds of agony. She groaned with every breath and clutched her sides.

'Ray,' said Earl, 'I think you might have some broken ribs. You need to be real careful moving.'

He helped her stand. Righting a chair, he gently eased her into it. Her mind was as much a mess as her body.

What the hell just happened?

Intruders had come in the night, beaten her, robbed her. Her Colt revolver and rifle were gone. As were the boxes of shells, and her bag of money hidden under the mattress. Most of her possessions looked like they'd been smashed out of pure spite. She had nothing left. Ray slumped in the chair; one arm crossed against her chest. Tears flowed freely, making rivers down her dust-streaked face. She felt despair in every cell of her body.

Why couldn't they have just killed me?

Fourteen

Ray lost track of time. The world around her faded in and out. Then she heard the pounding hooves of galloping horses, the shouts of men. She glanced at Earl; panic invaded her features. Had those monsters returned? Were there different men coming to beat and rob her — or worse? Earl strode to the door, shielding his eyes against the glare of the sun. To Ray's relief he turned to her, smiling reassurance.

'It's OK Ray, it's the Sheriff and a couple of deputies.'

Earl returned to Ray's side, placing a gentle hand on her shoulder.

'If it's ok with you Ray, I'll take myself for a walk. It won't do for the Sheriff to find me here. It'll raise more questions than answers.'

Ray placed her hand on top of Earl's, nodding OK.

Moments later she heard the Sheriff's voice.

'You in there Ray?' he boomed through the broken door. 'I'm coming in now. Don't want to see no gun pointing at me.'

The Sheriff's tall spare figure stood silhouetted in the doorway. He caught sight of Ray slumped on the chair and the chaos around her. In two strides he'd crossed the room and was kneeling in front of her, scrutinising the bruising and blood. Two deputies waited in the doorway, seemingly unwilling to cross the threshold.

'Jim, you head back into town and fetch the Doc,' the Sheriff snapped. 'Ain't no way she's fit to ride there herself.'

He spun round, snarling at them.

'Go on, now, quick!' he yelled. 'Bo, you come help me with Ray.'

Bo tentatively shuffled into the room. The Sheriff turned the bed upright and put the remains of the mattress on top, covering it with a blanket. He turned his attention to Ray hunched on the chair.

'Come on Bo, give me a hand with her.'

Bo sniffed and pulled a face.

Together, they helped her off the chair. Half-carrying her over to the bed, they gently laid her down. The Deputy wiped his hands on his breeches. He turned to the Sheriff keeping his voice low.

'She ain't none too clean boss, and this place stinks like it's well over ripe.'

The Sheriff straightened himself and took in the condition of the room.

'Yeah, well you can make yourself useful while we wait for the Doc and start cleaning up.'

The two men busied themselves gathering the fragments of the wooden table, and other broken items, dumping them in a pile outside. Bo avoided the sight of the injured woman on the bed as he worked. With the place cleaned up, as well as it could be, the Sheriff and Bo sat on the veranda awaiting Doc's arrival. The Sheriff slumped in the chair. His long legs stuck straight out in front, crossed at the ankles, hat tipped down shielding his eyes from the sun's glare. Bo stared straight ahead in the haze. He avoided facing the Sheriff as he spoke.

'Boss, you think there's truth in the rumours about her?'

'Not sure it's our job to listen to rumours boy,' muttered the Sheriff, still and quiet in his seat.

'She sure looks crazy to me.'

Bo glanced over his shoulder, half expecting to see Ray.

The Sheriff lifted the brim of his hat, glaring at Bo to make his point stick.

'Like I said son, it isn't our job to be listening to rumours. Least still spreading 'em. Our job's to uphold the law and that's what we're going to do. Regardless of what you think of that lady lying beaten up in there, she don't deserve what's happened to her and we're going to deal with that. So I suggest that you start working that brain on how we're going to do that, instead of chewing on town gossip.'

The Sheriff stood, raising his hand against the fierce sun. There was a dust cloud on the trail, two horses he figured at a guess.

'Anyhow Bo, Doc's coming now. Let's be dealing with him first, before we move onto the next thing.'

The Doc nodded to them, as he got off his horse, handing the reins to Jim. His movements were stiff and slow as he climbed the uneven steps up to the veranda.

'Jim here tells me Ray's hurt pretty bad, so I rode to be quicker. Something my old bones clearly don't appreciate. Can you tell me what happened?'

'Not sure Doc, except the obvious. She's been worked over and the cabin's got trashed. Seems they took what had value and the rest they broke.'

The Sheriff moved aside to allow Doc onto the veranda.

'We came out to check on her first thing, after we picked up the men that did this. Bob Wallace said he'd seen two men come into the saloon late last night. They filled up on whiskey and then took a room. Bob noticed one of them carrying Melvin Crow's rifle and he figured only one place they could have got that. He came over to the office and got me, while them two cowboys were still passed out sleeping off their whiskey.'

The Sheriff paused, glancing back towards the open cabin, gesturing inside.

'They had no shame about them at all. Seems hard to believe they'd be drinking their fill of whiskey and sleeping soundly seeing what they done to 'the crazy lady.' That's what they called her. Said they didn't even fuck her, 'cos she was stinking and crazy, and they didn't want to be cursed.'

He shook his head slowly.

'Anyways, them boys are in lock up now. Ain't had much chance to question them. Figured me and the boys should ride out and see Ray first. She ain't got no one else looking out for her.'

He nodded toward the shattered cabin door.

'Time you got about your business Doc. I'll leave Jim here with you. Me and Bo'll head back into town and see what those cowboys have to say for themselves.'

Gesturing to Bo, the Sheriff walked purposefully toward his horse, a frown creasing his forehead.

The Doc dragged a chair next to Ray's bed. He spent some time checking Ray's injuries. All the while she lay still, her breath shallow, sweating with the pain and humiliation of it all.

He spoke gently and with kindness.

'Well girl, you got yourself a good beating. But other than a couple of broken ribs it's mostly just bruising. Though some of that will be to your insides. You got a cut on your head, but it's not deep and don't need stitches. You're going to have a helluva headache for a few days. And you'll be sore as hell, but you'll be ok in a month, or two maybe. Or so I reckon. That's assuming there's no damage to your organs. Either way, you got to take things easy a while.'

The Doc paused, waiting for a response from Ray, but none came. She lay still and quiet. The Doc shrugged and continued.

'Ray, thing is, I don't advise staying out here by yourself. Not after what's happened. Not for a while at least.'

Ray turned her eyes to the Doc, saying nothing.

'I'm not sure,' he continued, 'how you're going to be able to look after yourself, specially with those ribs. Might be we need to see if there's a room in town for you, just till you're healed.'

Ray's head pounded and her body ached more than she thought was possible to bear. Her throat was dry and hurt like hell. When she tried to speak it cracked and rasped. Doc gave her water to sip. Eventually she said:

'I'm not going anywhere... that's what they want. Soon as I leave here... they'll be taking it all.'

'Girl, you're just as likely to die out here by yourself in this state, and then anyone who wants your land will come and take it. Best you get yourself to town. Sheriff'll make sure that your place is left alone. You can come back and get it straight when you're right.'

Silence fell between them. Ray shook her head.

The Doc hefted his bag and stood, bones creaking. There was resignation in his voice.

'OK Ray, I can't force you to do anything you don't want. I'll try and come out to see you in a few days. I sure hope you'll be bit better when I visit.'

Ray lay on the cot, each breath burning like swallowing hot coals fuelling the white-hot pounding behind her eyes. Her grip on her own body felt weak. Like any minute, she'd break away and fly again, leaving her damaged body behind.

She lay as still as she could, her breathing shallow and her eyes tight closed, willing herself to abandon her body. She lay like that for a long time. Finally she fell into a fitful sleep.

Fifteen

The Sheriff and his deputies idly watched the cowboys sleeping in the cell. Each prisoner with his hat over his face blocking out the light. Their snoring echoed round the office — a tuneless cacophony disturbing the peace of the morning.

The Sheriff turned to Bo.

'How about you make some coffee, boy. I think I'm going to need something to help me through questioning these two.'

He turned to Jim and pointed towards the door.

'And how about you head out and get me something to eat'.

The Sheriff sat at his desk. There was a steaming cup of coffee and a plate of sausage and beans in front of him. As he started to eat, he noticed the snoring had stopped. He glanced at the cell to see both cowboys awake. One still lay on the cot, the other was sitting, elbows on his knees, staring at him.

The Sheriff snorted.

'I'll be having my breakfast nice and quiet like. Then we'll discuss what you boys got up to last night.'

'Not sure what you're talking about,' came a rough, gravelled voice. 'But I'd sure appreciate something to eat. It's been a while and I'm damned hungry.' He turned to the man lying on his cot. 'I'm sure my brother could do with a bite, too.'

Jim's voice came from the side of the room.

'You might get yourself something to eat, once you've told the Sheriff what he needs to know, and after we decide what we're going to be doing with you. But right now, you just sit there with your mouth shut.'

The prisoner turned his head and glared at Jim. His face was hard and lined, with thin lips and scarring on his left cheek. He hawked and spat before replying.

'Deputy, I suggest you head out over to Mickleton's place.

Dwain'll vouch for us. We work for him. Well, we did until yesterday, when we decided to move on.'

The Sheriff continued eating his breakfast and sipping his coffee. He was taking his sweet time, savouring each bite, blowing steam from his mug before each sip. Silence settled back on the room while the Sheriff finished his meal.

Pete Mickleton appeared in the doorway.

'Sheriff, what's going on here?' he nodded towards the prisoners. 'Jim tells me these two attacked Ray Crow last night.'

The Sheriff wiped the last of the beans off his plate with a piece of bread. Putting it in his mouth, he raised his eyes to Pete. He chewed slowly and silently. Once he swallowed, he wiped crumbs from the front of his shirt. Making a point, taking his time. When he was done a humourless smile appeared on his face.

'Mighty good to see you Pete, wasn't expecting you. Right now, I'm in the middle of some business and I ain't got time for a chat.'

He picked his teeth, gesturing to the men in the cell.

'Need to question these boys, right now, and there ain't no place for you here when I'm doing that.'

'They worked for my brother till yesterday,' Pete said, crossing the room to the Sheriff's desk. 'They ain't no good, I can tell you that, and if they hadn't left of their own accord, my brother would have made 'em. They reckon they'd worked with cattle before, but I reckon they're only good for whoring and stealing.'

The scarred man jumped up and grabbed the cell bars.

'We worked for your brother, not you,' he spat. 'You don't know nothing about us.' He laughed turning to look at the man still laying silently on his cot. 'We might have done some stealing, but hell, at least we're not low enough to touch that crazy lady.'

Pete's face hardened and he leapt towards the cell. The Sheriff jumped up from his desk, his chair clattering to the floor. He stood between Pete and the prisoner.

'Pete,' he said, 'time for you to leave. You being here ain't doing no-one no good. I suggest you head over to Bob's place for a coffee, finish your business in town and go home.'

He turned to Jim.

'Deputy, see Pete out the door, and whilst you're doing it maybe you could refrain from talking law business to civilians.'

Pete stood rigid, staring at the men behind the bars. Jim

walked over placing a hand gently on his arm.

'C'mon Pete, let's walk outside.'

Pete turned wordlessly and followed Jim out of the office. As he reached the busy street the Sheriff began his interrogation.

'First things first gentlemen. Perhaps you could give me your names?'

He leaned on his desk, arms crossed, awaiting a response.

'My name's Cole,' said the man with the scar, he gestured to the other, stretched on the cot. 'And this here's my brother Audley.'

The other man lifted his hat by way of acknowledgement, eyes fixed on the ceiling.

The Sheriff walked over to the cell.

'Well, which one of you is going to tell me what happened at Ray Crow's place last night? We know you robbed her.'

He pointed to Ray's rifle propped up against the far wall and a pile of items next to it.

'As well as those guns, I expect what's left in that money pouch belongs to her, and those shells. And no doubt some of the food you boys was carrying.'

Cole went to speak, when Audley rose from the cot and raised a hand to stop him. There was a calm, cold expression on his face and his movements were slow and controlled like something deadly you'd find under a rock in the desert. The Sheriff reckoned he was ten years or so older than Cole. His face was tanned and heavily lined. Audley nodded toward Cole before speaking.

'He ain't my brother, not really. We just been together so long that we might as well be.'

His voice was deep and mellow, contrasting with the roughness of Cole's delivery.

'Now I won't deny that we robbed that lady, if you can call her that. More like a witch or something unnatural. It'd be pretty stupid to deny we done robbed her, what with you finding us with some of her stuff, but we needed some provisions and Dwain pointed us in that direction.'

The Sheriff's eyes narrowed.

'Are you telling me Dwain told you to go rob Ray Crow's place?'

Audley looked at Cole and they sniggered.

'I wouldn't say he told us to exactly, not in so many words. Thing is Sheriff, I ain't much good at taking orders from people, which is why we was leaving the Mickleton ranch. It's ok to have a job for a while, but then the orders start chaffing at me and my boy here, so we leave before it gets nasty. But Dwain said enough about that crazy lady, he might as well have told us her homestead was open for business. Truth be told, me and my boy thought we might get a little action whilst we were there. But even we weren't desperate enough for that.'

Cole spat before speaking.

'And that crazy bitch tried to kill me. Reckon we would have just robbed the place if she hadn't tried to shoot me. I managed to get the gun out the way, but then the bitch went crazy on me. Had no choice but to put her down.'

He turned to look at Audley.

'She's lucky we didn't kill her, ain't that right Audley?'

'Cole sure is right. When it comes down to it, we was just protecting ourselves.'

The Sheriff considered their words, then turned to Bo.

'Deputy, get these boys something to eat. I'll not have anyone starving in my jail.'

'So,' said Cole, 'you going to let us go, or what?'

'Not yet son, not yet. You might as well make yourself comfortable. We'll pick this up again tomorrow.'

With that he grabbed his hat and headed into the street.

Sixteen

5 years ago:

Ray paused from splitting firewood seeing Pete approaching. She smiled watching his horse's long, loping stride and swinging head. As he got closer, she saw the grin on Pete's face matching her own.

'Hey there stranger,' she yelled, 'what brings you here?'

Pete pulled his horse up to the wood pile. He leaned forward toward her, his forearm resting on his saddle horn.

'I'm checking the fence line twixt our ranch and your place, so I thought I'd skip across to see you as I'm hereabouts.'

Ray stood, waiting and smiling. Pete shook his head slightly. Sometimes he forgot that Ray needed things spelled out to her.

'So, I was thinking you might want to tack up that little pony of yours and come ride with me a while?'

Ray drove the hatchet deep into the chopping block. Wiping her sweat stained hands on the front of her dress she gave a whoop of excitement.

'I got lots of chores to do, but I reckon I could go. Ma and Pa said they had neighbourly business to attend to, so they won't even know I'm gone.'

Ray carried on talking, half to Pete and half to herself, as she skipped back to the barn to saddle up Rio. She wasn't sure what Ma would do if she got back and she wasn't here. But the excitement of riding out with Pete took over and she pushed the thought out of her mind. She tacked up Rio and led him out of the barn, grabbing her hat from a post on her way past and jamming it on her head to protect herself from the hot sun. She mounted and pulled up alongside Pete.

'My Rio might be little,' she said, looking up at him, 'but he's fast and sure, maybe even faster than that loping great beast you're sat on.'

'Is that a challenge? 'Cos if it is I'm sure it's one you ain't going to win!' Pete reined his horse about, spurring her into a canter away from the homestead, and out toward the ranch's southern fence line. Ray brought Rio up alongside. They loped along in a comfortable silence, the challenge already forgotten in the hard ground and hot sun.

After a while they brought the horses back to a walk, moving slowly along the fence line. Pete checked for damage that would allow the ranch's cattle to escape. It was Pete broke the silence.

'Tell me Ray, how old are you now?'

'Mmmm. Not all that sure. But I figure fifteen-year-old or so.'

'I did wonder, 'cos it's pretty hard to tell just by looking at you. You could be thirteen or twenny, it's difficult to say. But fifteen makes you two years younger'n me.'

He paused, checking a fence post with a kick before continuing.

'D'you an' your family go to church Ray, in town, on a Sunday.'

Ray shook her head.

Her shock of red hair caught the breeze.

'No, Ma and Pa don't go to church. Ma says, "God's in the land and the plants and the animals, he don't be needing a wooden church and he don't be needing our useless prayers."'

Ray laughed at her impression of her mother.

'My Ma and Pa don't go to church neither. I know they used to a long time ago, 'cos that's how come they started courting. But I don't ever remember going.'

He paused, allowing his next words time to settle, before he spoke them out loud.

'So Ray, I was wondering if you don't go to church, and you don't go into town much, then how is it that you'll find someone to court you?'

Pete guided his horse along the fence line in silence waiting for her reply. He looked back at her trailing him. She was staring up at the sky, her hand shielding her eyes from the glare of the sun.

'What're you so intent on, Ray?'

'Can you see the bird up there Pete', she said excitedly, rising in the saddle, 'the raven; can you see it?' She pointed to a speck in the distance. 'Isn't it beautiful, I can see all the colours in its feathers, red and green and gold, just watch it Pete.'

Pete looked up at a black speck flying in the distance. He could barely see the bird, let alone pick out the colours of its feathers. He shook his head, perplexed. Ray watched the bird for the longest while. Pete felt shut out. He shook his head and turned around, pointing back to the homestead.

'Come on Ray, probably best we're heading back now.'

When Ray and Pete arrived back, they dismounted and fetched water for the horses. After their mounts had their fill, Pete tied his horse up outside the cabin and Ray put Rio back in the barn, dropping her hat back on the post outside. She untacked him and put him away in his stall. Dust motes danced in shafts of sunlight streaming through gaps in the roof. Pete laughed as Ray swirled around like she was trying to catch them.

He knew he liked her, had a man's feelings for her. He'd met plenty other girls in town, but none like Ray. He found them silly, and way too prim, with their fancy costumes and high-toned attitudes. He couldn't imagine any of them living out on the ranch like his Ma did. Ray was different: beautiful, interesting and she had a real good way with animals.

He'd tried to talk to Pa about her, about courting her, but his father shut him down pretty quick every time. Pete wondered if it was because there was sometimes bad blood between him and Ray's Pa. Melvin was a gambler, often down on his luck. And Pete knew he could be slow to pay his debts. His own Pa lived for the ranch and his family. He told Pete and Dwain all the time that the ranch would be theirs one day when he'd gone, and he was going to make it as big and successful as he could before his passing. Pete wanted a family of his own one day. He and Ray were neighbours after all and it would make sense if him and Ray married someday. Then maybe along the line they could combine their spreads.

As he watched her playing Pete wondered why Ray was so different. It wasn't just the way she looked; it was the way she acted. Having a conversation with Ray was not like with anyone else. She saw the world differently and had a fresh way of relating to it. To him it made her special. Although some in town thought differently and used words like 'crazy,' or 'mad,' or worse. Ray's dance slowed. Soon she stood still gazing up at the light beams forcing their way through the roof. As the sun lit her hair it became burning red, like flames licking up from a fire. Pete approached. He reached out gently to touch her radiant hair, as he might to a newborn foal. She stood still and quiet, her gaze still fixed on the light. Pete wasn't sure she even knew he was there. He stroked her thick tresses surprised by their softness. Something was stirring in him like the pull of magnetic attraction. Pete edged closer, cupping the back of her head, pulling her toward him. His lips brushed hers, it felt like a burning fuse was running through his body. He closed his eyes and pulled her closer, pressing their lips together.

'Get away from my daughter!'

Pete froze.

Ray's Pa was at the barn doors, his silhouette, featureless and dark. Pete took a step back. Ray remained where she was, still smiling, eyes unfocussed. Pete went to speak.

'Mr Crow, Sir, I've been meaning...'

But Ray's Pa cut him off. Anger swelled his words till they filled the barn.

'You get away from my daughter, d'you hear! You're not welcome. Sneaking around here when we're gone, trying to take advantage of a child.'

He raised his rifle, aiming at Pete.

'I should gun you down like a varmint.'

Pete raised his hands, stepping further away from Ray.

He tried speaking again.

'Mr Crow, if you...

'Get the hell out of my barn — now!'

He was trembling, face reddening, sweat beading his sun-burnished forehead. Ray's Ma appeared, her cool manner like water on flames. She took hold of her husband's arm and gently eased the rifle down.

'You come here boy,' she said to Pete.

She beckoned him towards her. He walked unsteadily toward the barn door — hands raised. As he passed Ray's glowering Pa, he felt palpable waves of anger radiating from him. Pete was uncertain he'd make it to the door without being shot. Lena took a step forward and took Pete by the arm, escorting him through the doorway.

He glanced back at Ray, she hadn't moved. He longed to say goodbye but feared angering her Pa any further.

Lena led Pete back to his horse.

'You should head on back, Pete,' she said sadly, shielding him as he mounted.

'I know you have feelings for Ray, and I know you've been out here before spending time with her. But I'm telling you son, she is not the girl for you. Don't matter that you think she is, I'm telling you she ain't.'

She looked up at Pete imploringly, silently pleading for him to understand.

'And I'm telling you, that if you come out here again to see her and my husband finds out, he will shoot you. You've had your warning. Do you hear me, son?'

Pete nodded before speaking carefully chosen words.

'Thing is Ma'am, I was thinking to court Ray proper like, formal you know?'

Lena shook her head vigorously.

'Pete, you need to get that thought out of your head right now! You're a good man and you'll find yourself another woman in town. Now I know you don't want to take advantage of Ray. But that's what you'd be doing. So please Pete, listen to what I'm telling you. Ride on home and don't come back here.'

Lena took a step back. Pete reined his horse around and headed away from the homestead. He'd not gone more than fifty paces, before looking back over this shoulder. Lena's stiff-backed stance and rigid features told him it was no use arguing. He lowered his head and made for home.

If he'd looked back again he'd have seen Lena watching him, until he was nothing but a speck in the distance.

Seventeen

Ray lay in her bed watching the sun begin its climb. Pink and orange shards of light sprang over the horizon. To her it was like the sun had burst the crust of the earth, its fragments lighting up the dawn sky. The air was still and quiet; the chill of the night lingered until the sun brought warmth to the world. It wouldn't be long before its heat would overtake the cabin.

Ray closed her eyes and uttered a fervent prayer. They needed rain. They'd needed rain for months and she felt keenly that her life might just depend on it. She longed for the sound of fat raindrops bouncing on the roof, splattering into the dust, turning it into thick brown mud. She imagined the roots of the corn greedily sucking up the deluge, bringing new life to their wilted brown leaves, swelling the stunted cobs. The rain would wash away the stink of everything; it would herald a fresh start.

Ray blinked to see Earl standing over her, smiling. He'd been a constant comforting presence since the Doc left. She'd felt safe with him there, even with the broken door opening the cabin to the world outside. Earl offered prayers and danced for her. The rhythmic sound of his slippered feet soothed and calmed her. As he danced, she would hear birds gathering outside the cabin. Their calls, echoing to the hills, blended with the pounding of Earl's steps, made music that called to her. It invited her soul up into the sky to soar on the cleansing wind and escape the world of men. When he'd completed his dance, she'd close her eyes, feeling Earl's hand on her forehead, cool and reassuring. She'd drift to sleep, leaving the pain and fear behind.

It had only been a day since those men had invaded her cabin, but it felt like a lifetime. Already she could feel herself healing, the bones of her ribs knitting together, the bruised knots in her back softening. She felt somehow lighter, and her worries and fears were kept at bay. She looked around the cabin, at shattered door, and the mirage world outside.

'Earl, we've got to get that door fixed. I don't know how, but we gotta do it somehow.'

Earl smiled ruefully.

'That door is the least of our worries, he said. 'It didn't keep out those thieving woman-beating bastards did it? No, food is by far the most pressing issue. I found some flour they missed so we can make biscuits. And there's some meat still hanging in the barn. But that's all you got. It's not going to keep you going for long. And you've no money to buy more, either.'

Earl squatted next to Ray and looked her in the eye.

'You think things were tough before? Well girl, they just got a whole lot harder. You need to decide whether you stay here and tough it out, or take your chances in town. If you stay, there's no guarantee you'd make it. Or you could come with me, fly away from here?'

Ray smiled weakly.

'Away where Earl?' she said. 'I don't even know where you come from.'

'I can help you Ray, you just have to ask. I can take you to someplace safe, away from all this suffering. Away from the dead weight of this earth. You just have to let go and I'll take you there.'

Earl took hold of Ray's hand. She felt his strength and his unconditional love. She could go with him and leave everything behind. It would be a fresh start.

'Ray?'

Someone was calling from outside.

'Ray!'

She turned her head to the door. Outside in the heat haze a man was dismounting from his horse. She held her breath as he stepped onto the veranda. He hesitated before the remains of the door. Then, removing his hat, he stepped in. Ray looked to Earl, but he was gone. Turning back, she recognised Pete. Pain returned.

Pete blanched as he quietly approached her bed.

'Jesus Ray, you're in a helluva state,'

She groaned. What was happening? She could feel her bones grinding. Every breath stabbed at her broken ribs. Every muscle was agony. Her head was pounding like a jack hammer. Fear flooded back.

Pete looked at the emaciated woman lying on the bed. He could hardly believe it was Ray. She was bruised, bloody and covered in filth. She couldn't look after herself. Even if the cabin was squared away and she had sufficient food, she'd be hard pressed to fetch wood, light a fire, or cook herself something. He doubted she'd last more than a day or two if he left her. Pete reached out a hand and tentatively felt her forehead — she was burning up.

'Just hang in there Ray, OK?' he said, 'I'll be back.'

Pete rode hard to the Mickleton ranch and burst through the ranch house door. Dwain was hunched at the table eating dinner; Sally was at the stove fixing a pot of coffee.

'Where the hell have you been?' snarled Dwain through a mouthful of beans. 'I've been out checking the cattle myself this afternoon, and I got the boys fixing the bottom fence, and you're nowhere to be found.'

Pete hung his hat on a peg by the door.

'Went into town like I told you. Then I checked on Ray Crow,'

'What the hell you done that for,' said Dwain angrily, pushing his empty plate away. 'She ain't your responsibility, this place is your responsibility. What happens to that girl ain't your lookout.'

Pete took a deep breath, looking first to Sally, and then to his brother, struggling to calm his voice.

'Hell Dwain, d'you know what happened to her? Those two assholes, Cole and Audley, done over the Crow place and gave Ray one helluva beating. Seems like they're insinuating you put them up to it. Hell, even if you didn't tell them, they still did it and they worked for us! That girl is pretty beat up and if she don't get no care, then she's going to die and that is my lookout. Hell, it's our lookout. We brought that on her, one way or another.'

Dwain leapt up, knocking his chair over. He spun toward Pete, anger blazing in his eyes.

'That girl is one crazy pale-ass bitch. Her family kept her locked up her whole life, and for good reason. Now her Ma and Pa are dead, I reckon she's better off that way too. She ain't no good to no-one. With her in the ground we can put that land to good use.'

Pete clenched his fist and went to fly at Dwain.

Sally stepped between them, voice shaking.

'Please boys, you know I don't like fighting in this house.'

The brothers glared at each other until Dwain broke the

silence.

'It's ok Ma,' he said softly, eyes fixed on Pete. 'We ain't going to fight. We promised when Pa died there wouldn't be no violence in this house.'

Dwain put his arm around Sally, gently settling her into a chair. Pete took a deep breath to calm himself. Hands shaking, he poured some coffee. When he spoke, his voice was calm and firm.

'I'm going to take some food and head out to the Crow place for a few days. Someone's got to look after the girl and there ain't no-one else.'

Dwain opened his mouth to protest, but a glare from Sally silenced him.

'You can't be going out and living at the Crow place with the girl by yourself,' she said. 'It's not seemly. How are you going to take care of her, dress her wounds? No, you're a man and she's a woman; you can't do that to someone who's not your wife. Besides that, we need you here at the ranch.'

She fixed her gaze on the tabletop, taking a slow breath before speaking.

'You'll have to bring her out here. I'll take care of her, until she's recovered enough to go back home.'

Dwain slammed his hand on the table.

'Ma, what in the hell are you saying! We don't want that crazy bitch out here! And what about that debt? You said yourself that we need that land. This drought is killing us here Ma, our cattle don't have enough grass. We'll all be starving if we don't do something.'

'Son, I full know what problems we got. But Ray's Ma helped me out once, a long time ago when you boys were little, and I can't sit by knowing that girl is dying a slow death, out there by herself. I know getting some Crow land would be the best thing for us. So, while the girl is staying here, why don't you start moving some of our cattle onto the top of her land. She's got crops down by the cabin so leave them be, just use the top ground for grazing. It won't hurt her none and it'll help us a little.'

'But Ma, said Dwain, 'that girl ain't...'

Sally raised her hand before he could finish. She stood tall and proud, her features set hard in her face. But when she spoke her words were soft.

'Dwain, you ain't going to change my mind and I don't want you challenging me in my own kitchen. This won't be forever, and it may be that we can all get to know each other a little. Could be when that happens, Ray won't be so against us with regards to the land.'

Dwain nodded sulkily.

'OK Ma, but I don't want nothing to do with that crazy bitch.'

He glared at Pete as he righted his chair, before pouring himself coffee and stomping out onto the veranda. When he'd gone Sally slumped back in her chair.

'Pete, it's too late to head back there now, it'll be dark by the time you get there. Why don't you get yourself some good sleep and head on out to the Crow place first thing in the morning.'

'Ok, Ma.'

Pete stood and kissed the top of her head. Then he headed outside. Sally rose to clear the table, blocking out the uncivil murmurings of her sons outside. Her thoughts returned to Ray. She wondered if she was doing the right thing, taking her into her home. She remembered Lena's face looking down at her a long time ago. Remembered the kindness and gentleness that flowed from Lena's hands. She owed her for that. No way she'd let her daughter die all alone.

Eighteen

Ray lay in the back of the wagon as it bumped its way across the plain. She was burning under the sun's heat and every turn of the wheels brought renewed pain, surely her bones had been torn from their sockets. She felt like an amalgam of parts, disconnected yet linked by pathways of pain. She didn't understand why Pete was taking her to his place. He said it was his Ma's idea but she didn't believe him.

Why would Sally Mickleton do anything to help her?

She grimaced, pain in even a flicker of expression. Fragmented thoughts started connecting in her head.

That was it, if she wasn't on her land protecting it, then they could take it over. But what would they do when she'd recovered? Maybe they planned on her not recovering!

Fear rose, curdling with the pain. Her breathing was reduced to short gasps, her chest tightening. She screwed up her eyes. And there was Earl's dark face smiling down at her.

'It's ok Ray,' he spoke gently, 'it's going to be ok, have faith.'

Her breathing slowed, pain began to subside. Earl's cool hand once more soothed her forehead. The wagon's violent motion became the rocking of a cradle. She felt calmness descending, and sleep taking her over. She was a bird circling high in the sky, riding the thermals, feeling the cool air flow through her flight feathers. Her eyes were impossibly sharp, taking in the contours of the land and the slightest movement of the creatures on its surface. She circled effortlessly, until the wagon rocked to a stop at the Mickleton ranch.

Ray heard voices but couldn't make out what was being said. She wanted to open her eyes, but it was like they were sewn shut. Strong arms lifted her into the cool interior of the house. She sunk into the billowy softness of a bed. Cool, damp womanly hands caressed her face before the void of sleep engulfed her. When she next woke it was in a nightdress, covered by a single blanket. The sun was low in the sky, casting a pink light in the room. She raised her hands to her face. They were spotless, even her nails had been scrubbed. Her pale skin shone in the light. She raised her arm to her face and sniffed. She smelt different somehow. Clean.

'You smell like soap,' spoke a woman's quiet voice. 'I put some herbs in when I make it so it smells nice. The boys don't appreciate it, but I do.'

Ray turned her head to see a tall woman with long, grey hair standing by the door. She wore a dress with an apron over the top. Both looked clean, but well-worn and Ray noticed she wore strong boots on her feet.

'I cleaned you up real good and that was no mean feat, 'cos I don't think you'd seen water for some time.' She let out a small laugh. 'But there ain't nothing I can do with that hair.'

Ray reached up tentatively with one hand and felt her head. Same as always. Thick knotted ropes.

'You can't wash it like that. And I think there might even be critters living in it. Best thing in my opinion is to shave it off, but I didn't want to do that when you was sleeping.'

Ray's eyes connected with those of the unknown woman. She saw tiredness and kindness in her grey eyes. This was not the woman she was expecting. She opened her mouth to speak, but the words cracked and broke as they tried to crawl out of her dry throat. The woman approached the bed. Taking a cup of water, she gently lifted Ray's head and helped her sip. As she lay back down Ray again went to speak, but the woman spoke first.

'My name is Sally Mickleton,' she said. 'I knew your Ma, not well you understand, but I knew her. She helped me once, when I desperately needed it. Was a long time ago, some twenty years maybe. I never saw her again after that, but I feel I owe her something. Ain't nothing I can do for her now she's passed, but I figured I could do something for you.'

Sally turned her head to the door. Ray heard men's indistinct voices and boots scraping on the floor.

'I need to feed my boys,' said Sally, 'I'll bring you something to eat, when we're done.'

Ray's eyes fluttered shut. Sally left the room, closing the door quietly behind her.

It didn't feel like long before Sally was back in the room. She was carrying a bowl of stew and more water. She helped Ray to sit up, so she could eat. Ray tentatively dipped the spoon in the stew. She couldn't remember when she'd last eaten, but she didn't feel hungry. She put a small piece of meat in her mouth and chewed. It was tough but tasty. She swallowed the juices, feeling them flow down her throat into her belly. At first, she felt her stomach roll and thought it might refuse the food. But in an instant it settled and demanded more. Ray hunched over the bowl and put spoonful after spoonful of meat and broth into her mouth, until the bowl was empty. Sally watched her without speaking. When Ray was finished, she took the bowl. Ray settled back down and closed her eyes. Sally watched her a while as she slept. She tossed from time to time, mumbling incoherently.

Sally stepped out onto the veranda. Both boys were sitting with coffee watching the end of the day cross the sky. They stopped talking when they saw Sally. She looked from one to the other, before speaking.

'OK boys, so what do you have to say? Seems, you both got some words sitting heavy on you.'

Pete looked across at Dwain, his face set hard. Dwain spoke slowly, his voice strained but controlled.

'Ma, I just ain't understanding what's going on here. First you say you want to take that debt, after old man Crow shot Pa dead. Now you're caring for the girl, when all we had to do was wait for her to up and leave, or die, then we could have had that land all legal like, fair and square.'

Pete turned his head to look at his Ma, waiting for her answer. But when she replied, she looked straight ahead, avoiding both of them, speaking into the distance.

'Boys, I loved your Pa in my own way. Goddam, he could be a cruel man, but he provided for us and he didn't deserve to die in the street. We do need more land, or money to buy feed for the cattle, but we don't need it at the expense of the life of that girl. She ain't done no-one any harm.'

Dwain looked up at Sally.

'I think she's crazy Ma. She sure looks crazy as hell. I don't understand her and I don't like what I don't understand. I think she could just up and kill someone one day. And how come she looks like she does? She looks like a ghost. And those eyes of hers, they don't look natural. And her hair, all red like rusted wire. There's all kinds of rumours about where she comes from. Some say she's the child of the devil.'

Pete laughed.

'That's a crock of shit, she ain't nothing but a girl.'

'Well, how do you explain her colouring, huh?' Answered Dwain. 'I ain't never seen nobody look like that.'

'Well jeez, I don't know,' responded Pete. 'And I don't see why it bothers you so much.'

Both boys turned to Sally.

'Ma?' said Dwain.

Sally gave both her boys a smile.

'Boys, I don't rightly know. I only met Lena Crow a few times and she never mentioned she had a child. I do remember a long time ago, your Pa telling me that Lena and Melvin had a little girl, out at their place. He saw her. She were only a young'un but he said there seemed something strange about her. I always wondered.' She shook her head sadly.

Pete turned his gaze toward the setting sun and thought about Ray. He remembered when he used to visit her, out at her place when she was a girl. He remembered her pale skin and pale blue eyes and how shiny her long red hair was. She looked exotic, so different from all the farm girls, or the girls in town. She could ride a horse like a man, and she had fire in her eyes, and when he was with her, his heart beat faster. He remembered how her Pa had run him off the land. He'd pointed that gun at him and looked him in the eye and swore that if he ever saw him on their land again, he'd kill him. Pete didn't doubt Melvin for a second. He'd always wondered after that whether he'd done the right thing by staying away. Maybe he should have gone back and tried to talk to Melvin, maybe tried harder to court Ray, formal-like. He'd tried to talk to his Pa about it at the time, but he'd got angry and told him to leave the Crow family alone. He'd threatened to beat him, if he heard he was mixing with them. So Pete had done what everyone seemed to want him to do, and he stayed away. Now his Pa was dead, and so were Melvin and Lena Crow, and Ray was lying beat up in a cot in his Ma's room. Pete shook his head.

Life sure could be crazy mixed up sometimes.

Pete realised they were sitting in silence and saw Dwain glaring at him.

'Well boy, what have you got to say?' Dwain spoke sharply.

'Sorry, what did you say?' answered Pete, shaking the fog out of his head.

'Ma says one of us should go out and fix up the Crow place, just in case any low-lifes find it, they might think it's been abandoned. I said you should do it. You can take one of the new boys with you. If you head out early tomorrow, you could be back in time for dinner.'

Pete nodded, having trouble clearing the past from his head.

'Sure Dwain, I can do that.'

Nineteen

The following morning, after breakfast, Dwain rode off to check on the cattle. Pete loaded up the cart with supplies and headed out to the Crow homestead with one of the ranch hands. Sally made a plate of breakfast and took it to Ray. She found her sitting up in bed looking out the window.

'How you feeling this morning, girl?'

'OK,' muttered Ray, eyeing up the plate of food hungrily.

Sally smiled, handing her the plate.

'Well you must be starting to feel a little better if you're hankering after food.'

When Ray had finished eating, Sally took a seat next to the bed and went to place a hand on Ray's forehead. Ray shrank away from her, fear in her eyes. Sally was shocked. She paused before speaking.

'Girl, I just wanted to gauge your temperature, so as to check you're healing OK. I'm not going to hurt you.'

Ray remained still and her eyes locked onto Sally's. Reaching slowly, like she would to a newborn calf, Sally placed her hand on Ray's forehead. Pleased to feel it dry and cool. No sign of fever. She was sure that once her bones knit, and bruises faded, she'd be fine.

'Maybe we could shave that hair off today. It's not healthy like that. It'll grow back before you know it — what d'you think?'

Ray nodded.

It was just hair.

Sally helped Ray sit in a chair at the table in the main room. She brought in a small shard of mirror and propped it up against a coffee pot, so Ray could see herself. It was a long time since Ray had looked in a mirror and she didn't recognise the person reflected at her. Her hands reached up to touch the mass of hair sticking out from her head. It was red, and grey with dirt, and felt rough to the touch. The long, thick and twisted skeins, looked like they were knitted together with grease and dirt. Underneath the hair, her skin was pale and her eyes sunken. Her cheekbones stood out, casting their own shadows. Ray's eyes moved to the top of the mirror. And there, close behind her, was Earl. She moved to turn in her seat, pleased to see him, but he shook his head, finger to his lips, sshhhhh. She smiled back secretively, until Sally stepped into view, placing a bowl of hot water and a bar of soap on the table.

'Here, let's put this cloth round your shoulders so we don't get you too wet and covered in hair,' she said, smiling. 'We'll get rid of this mess, and you'll see, it'll grow back in no time. I'm used to shaving my boy's hair. Seems like I'm having to do it every couple of weeks.'

Sally picked up a large knife from the table. Taking one of the thick red ropes, she cut it off close to Ray's head. One by one, she hacked them off. Some of them were thick and heavy, and some light and soft to the touch. As she cut she placed them on the table, building a pile of matted hair. The two women remained silent. As Sally worked Ray watched Earl's reflection in the mirror. He danced and smiled, weaving patterns in the air with his hands. Ray watched the air swirling, following Earl's hands, shining dust motes twinkling between his fingers. It wasn't long before Sally had cut off all the ropes. Now just the stumps stuck up from Ray's head.

'Well, I ain't never seen such a sight,' laughed Sally, shaking her head. She picked up another cloth and dipped it in warm water, before she lathered it up with the soap. Then she rubbed the cloth over Ray's head, coating the stumps with the greasy soap. She took up a razor and began carefully shaving Ray's head. Bit by bit, she scraped, soaping and shaving, until finally all the stumps had gone and Ray's head was completely bald.

'There you go girl. It'll feel mighty strange for a time, but you're clean, and you ain't got no vermin living on your head now. That's something to be thankful for.'

Ray checked herself in the mirror, turning her head this way and that. The dome of her head looked strange without hair, the smooth white skin shining. Her sunken eyes, piercing blue, belied the anxiety that was her constant companion.

She saw Earl in the mirror, flapping his arms, pretending to fly. She laughed, a deep throaty laugh. She raised her arms in imitation of Earl and flapped them like a bird.

'What on earth you laughing at girl?'

Sally finished drying off the bowl and turned to see Ray in front of the mirror flapping her arms.

'Damn girl,' she said laughing, 'have you done gone lost your mind?'

Ray turned to Sally; the smile refused to leave her face. As Sally met Ray's eyes she felt the breath leave her body on a wave of fear. The bowl dropped from her hands, thudding to the cabin floor.

The rest of Sally's day passed in a blur. She performed her regular chores with no conscious thought. Her body in the present, her mind stuck unwillingly in the past. She could sense Ray's presence in her room. The air in the ranch house felt uncommonly oppressive. She was relieved when her boys returned. The familiar smell of their sweat, and the rough sound of their voices settled her nerves. She immersed herself in the nightly routine of feeding the family, taking comfort from their presence.

The sound of hooves outside broke into the evening. Pete and Dwain looked at each other, questioning, before standing and making their way to the door.

'You expecting someone?' Pete asked Dwain.

'Uh, uh,' Dwain shook his head. Both men walked out on the veranda. Sheriff Boone and Deputy Jim came riding up. They hitched their horses to the rail and climbed the steps to the house. Sheriff removed his hat, nodding politely, at the brothers.

'Boys, we'd like a little talk with you about the incident out at the Crow place.'

The Sheriff craned his head looking past them into the cabin and smiled.

'Mmmhh, is that fresh coffee I smell. Sure would be nice to have a cup while we talk.'

Dwain turned to Pete.

'Go see Ma and get the Sheriff and Jim some coffee.'

'Understand you've got Ray Crow staying out here, which is mighty convenient for me, 'cos I'd sure like a word with her too.'

The Sheriff stood against the veranda rail, hands in the pockets of his jeans, smiling amiably at Dwain.

They stood in silence, until Pete came out onto the veranda carrying two cups of coffee, followed by Sally.

'Sally,' said Sheriff Boone, smiling, 'mighty fine to see you. I hope I'm finding you well?'

Sally returned his smile. She wasn't comfortable with him here. Not once in her life had the presence of a lawman been for any good reason.

'What d'you want with my boys?' she asked nervously.

'Well Ma'am, I need to have a chat with Dwain here about the attack on Ray Crow. Now, I still have those felons in my jail, and I need to understand whether to let them on their way, or have them collected by the Marshall, when he comes through town shortly.'

He paused eyeing Dwain and Pete carefully. His gaze settled on Dwain.

'You remember those boys don't you Dwain? Cole and Audley? Well they're getting a little fed up sitting in my jail eating beans twice a day. After a little sweating time, they told me you pointed them by way of the Crow place on their way out of town. Seems like you might have slipped them a few extra coins, as a parting gift, when they left your ranch.'

Sally turned to Dwain looking shocked.

She turned to the Sheriff.

'My boy wouldn't do that Sheriff. No sir. I'm not saying he wouldn't get into a bit of trouble himself, but he wouldn't do something like that. Dwain, tell the Sheriff.'

Dwain squared his shoulders, glaring at the lawman.

'Come on now Sheriff, you going to believe those two crooks or me?' He paused, shaking his head. 'I don't know what evidence you got that I might have done such a thing. Other than the word of two fellas, that I let go from my ranch.'

Dwain let his words hang in the air before continuing.

'But I'll say it out loud, so you get the message. I sure as hell didn't point them in the direction of the Crow place, and the only coin I gave them was what was owing when they left.' The Sheriff turned to Pete.

'You got anything to say, boy?

Pete shook his head.

'No sir, 'cept to say that I never heard my brother say nothing to those two assholes about Ray Crow. Saying that, Ray did come over to our place pretty riled up after the death of her pony. Cole and Audley were here when she did. Maybe that's when they seen her and decided they'd visit her place on their way. Or maybe they just saw her homestead when they was riding out.'

He shrugged.

'I don't know why they did what they did, but it weren't nothing to do with me or my brother.'

Silence fell on the veranda as Sheriff Boone sipped his coffee. After a minute he turned to Jim.

'What else was it that Cole said, Jim? I can't quite remember.'

'Well boss, he said something about Dwain taking rat poison out to the Crow place.'

'That's bullshit!' shouted Dwain.

'Well, that's what Cole is saying Dwain,' continued Jim. 'Seems like you were willing to do anything to get your hands on that land. Seems to me…'

Sheriff Boone jumped in.

'That'll do now, Jim. We don't want to go assuming things here. So, I'm going to ask you a simple question Dwain. Did you poison Ray Crow's oats?'

Dwain spoke through gritted teeth.

'No sir, I did not.'

'And Dwain, did you ask, or hell, even suggest, to Cole and Audley that they should pay Ray Crow a visit on their way out of town?'

'No sir, I did not.'

The Sheriff turned to Sally, who was standing straight with her hands clutching at the fabric of her apron. Her features were blank, but her eyes spoke of worry. He smiled reassurance and spoke kindly to her.

'Sally, I'm just doing my job here. I don't want to cause you any distress, but where there are accusations, I got to look into them.'

Sally nodded, but her face stayed set.

'Now I understand Ray is here. Might I have a word with her?'

Sally took a breath before speaking.

'Sheriff,' she said, her voice tight. 'I'll have to see whether she's up to talking. Her injuries are getting better by the day, but she's not always communicating well. She don't speak much and… Well, sometimes, she don't seem to be quite right, if you get what I'm saying.'

The Sheriff nodded and sipped his coffee.

'It's OK, Sally, perhaps you could go and see if Ray is feeling up to a chat, and I'll just wait out here with the boys.

'It's fine. I'll talk with the Sheriff.'

They all turned to see Ray standing in the doorway.

'Goodness girl, you should be in bed,' exclaimed Sally, as she hurried over to her. The Sheriff turned to Ray, taking in her strange appearance. She was thinner than the last time he'd seen her. Her shaved head gave her an otherworldly appearance

Christ! The girl looks half crazy.

Ray stood statue still, arms hanging loosely by her sides, as Sally fussed about, wrapping her in a shawl to cover her nightdress.

'Perhaps Sally, you might want to take Ray inside and get her dressed while me and the boys chew the fat.'

Sally led Ray back into the cabin. The Sheriff looked at Dwain and Pete. Dwain's face had been a picture of revulsion, as he looked at Ray. She disgusted him clearly, but the Sheriff had also noticed a hint of fear in Dwain's eyes. He nodded inwardly.

Yep, men sure feared what they didn't understand.

He turned to look at Pete who seemed to have other issues with her appearance. If anything, the look on his face had been of concern. There was no fear there, but there was something else. The Sheriff couldn't quite put his finger on it, but if he had to guess he would say desire. Yes, that was it. Pete looked at Ray, as if he desired her. He shook his head again.

Well, well, there ain't nothing crazier than folk.

Inside the cabin Sally took Ray back into the bedroom.

'Now girl, let's get some clothes for you. I think you'll be fine with one of my dresses. It'll be a little big for you, cos you're thinner than a cattle prod, and a little short, but it'll do.'

'I don't want to wear a dress,' answered Ray. 'I want my breeches.'

'I'm sorry Ray, but I had to throw them away. Besides they was just underclothes.'

Ray's face was fixed, her lips set in a straight line.

'I'm not wearing no dress.' Sally looked closely at Ray. She had the body of a man. Slim hips and no breasts to speak of.

'Well, you'll have to wear something of my husband's then. I've still got some of his clothes in here, although I dare say they'll be too big for you.'

She opened a trunk and pulled out a pair of old trousers and a faded brown shirt with patches sewn over old holes. After digging around in the trunk a little more, she found a leather belt. She handed the pile to Ray.

'I'll just wait outside, you get dressed now.'

When Sally was gone Ray pulled on the clothes, tucking the shirt into the pants and tightening the belt around her waist. She rummaged in the old trunk, finding a leather waistcoat, which she slipped over the shirt. She came across a black hat. She pulled it out of the trunk, running her fingers around the edge of the brim, before placing it on her head. It fit snuggly over the dome of her bald head. She stepped out into the main room of the cabin. Sally had waited. As she appeared in the doorway, Sally's breath froze, and her blood turned to ice. All she could see in front of her was a tall pale man, all limbs and bone, with pale blue bloodshot eyes. She fought to squash old memories rising deep where she'd buried them.

'Go on girl,' she said softly, 'go see the Sheriff.'

As Ray left, she sat down on a chair, dropping her head into her hands.

The men on the veranda looked up as Ray stepped outside. She moved awkwardly as if her limbs were strange to her. Every so often she winced as pain caught her out. She stood away from the men, leaning against the wall of the cabin. She angled the brim of her hat to cast a shadow across her face. There was an uncomfortable silence as the group took in her appearance. Sheriff Boone slowly and deliberately took a cigar out of his pocket and lit it. Without taking his eyes off Ray, he jerked his head towards Dwain and Pete.

'Say Jim, why don't you and the boys there take a short walk while I have a talk with Ray here.'

When the three men were out of hearing, the Sheriff spoke directly to Ray. 'Ray would you like to take a seat; I'm guessing you're still hurting pretty bad.'

'I'm OK, Sheriff. Thank you.'

'Well, you're looking a lot better than I expected you too. But I think you're a long way from healed.'

He grabbed two chairs and pulled one over next to Ray, and sat on the other. 'Here Ray, take a seat, while we talk.'

When they sat Ray tipped her hat back so she could look

directly at the Sheriff. Her eyes were bright, feverishly bright, and her gaze was penetrating.

'Ray I don't want to bring up unpleasant memories, but I do need to decide what to do with those two guys in my jail.' He paused, leaving room for Ray to speak, but she stayed silent. 'I can let them on their way with an order to leave town and say that two weeks in my jail is punishment enough for what they done. Or I can hand them to the Marshall when he arrives next week.'

He paused taking a draw on his cigar.

'But the thing is that I just got their word against Dwain's that this was nothing more than two drifters looking to make a quick buck. I don't think anyone's going to take the word of those two over a reputable rancher like Dwain Mickleton. No doubt too, that the Marshall will want you to come into town to take a statement from you, before he takes them boys away. Now, I don't know what you think about that?'

Ray heard the Sheriff's words floating on the breeze around her. She could remember the moment the men crashed into her cabin. She could remember the beating. The nightmares were still with her. But often it seemed like it was happening to someone else and she was floating above, watching it unfold beneath her. She looked at the Sheriff and simply shrugged.

'Ray, you got to give me something here. Now, I'm just of a mind to let them go. I know what they did to you was wrong, but you'll get your stuff back, and you'll heal. I can get my deputies to see them out of town and they'll not be back. But you're the one they put the beating on, so I think you ought to have a say in what happens.'

Ray closed her eyes feeling the late afternoon sun on her face. The Sheriff's words were now buzzing around her like flies. She pictured the face of the man she'd looked at across her cabin. She remembered that face from when she was laying on the floor with him kicking her. She tried to imagine what his face would look like if it was hit by a bullet from her gun; she could imagine blood and bone exploding like firecrackers.

'You should let them go, Sheriff. I don't want to talk to no-one about it. Just want to forget it happened and go back to my homestead.'

Ray stood and walked back into the cabin.
She needed to talk to Earl.

Twenty

Ray hauled on her boots. With uncertain steps she limped over to the barn. Pain still jarred when she walked. But if she took it slow, concentrating on gently putting one foot in front of the other, she could walk off the pain. Her chest ached and it still hurt to breathe. Her belly was covered in purple and yellow bruises, and she could feel swellings in her bony back. And her head still throbbed if she sat for too long or stood up too quickly.

But it felt so good to be moving, to feel the heat of the sun and the fresh air after being cooped up in Sally Mickleton's bedroom. She smiled as she stepped into the cool barn and took in the familiar smell of the animals. There were horses tethered in the barn, and there was Rain.

Pete must have brought him over.

She was grateful. She leant against his flank, feeling his hair against her skin and his warmth flowing through him. After a while, she felt a hand gentle on her back. She turned to see Earl, his characteristic smile and kind eyes a welcome sight. A smile spread across her face. She'd not seen him for days and sorely missed him.

'I thought you'd left,' she said. 'I was sad not to have said goodbye. I've missed you.'

'Ah well, I did leave. I had things to do and I knew you were in good hands. Sally cares about you. You have a connection. But I'm back now.'

He moved close and took her in his arms. She felt his energy joining with hers. As she relaxed the pain drifted away. She took a step back.

'Earl,' she said, 'I don't know what to make of all this. Don't know why Sally is taking care of me. She says it's 'cos my Ma took care of her once, but it don't make sense to me. And she tells me that Pete's looking after my homestead. Honestly, I think it's part of a plan to take my land, but I don't see how. I don't see things clearly no more.'

Ray turned back to Rain, laying her hands on his back. As she spoke her voice was muffled by her closeness to him.

'And Earl, there's those two cowboys. The ones that broke into my place. Sheriff said yesterday he's probably going to let them go.'

After a few moments Ray stepped away from Rain. She paced alongside him shaking her head, gathering her thoughts before turning back to Earl.

'I told the Sheriff to let them go. But I don't know, I really don't know. Don't want to talk to the Marshall or anyone about what happened. Not even think about what they did. I just want to forget. But I dream about it Earl. Every night I dream about those men and I hate what they did to me. I hate them for making me feel this way. They need to pay for what they did to me.'

Ray shook her head to clear the confusion.

'What should I do Earl?' she whispered.

Earl gripped her shoulder. She felt his composure steadying her and her breathing eased.

'Ray, why don't you go and speak to the Sheriff again. Your rifle and gun, your money, it's all at the Sheriff's office, remember he told you. Why don't you ride into town and pick up your things, if you're feeling up to it? And if those cowboys are still in jail, you'll see them. Maybe when you do, you'll know what to do.'

Ray nodded. Earl made sense as usual. That's just what she'd do. She'd ride into town and see the Sheriff. She'd look those men in the eye and decide what she wanted then. No longer would she let other folk make decisions for her.

She'd take control.

'Girl, where on earth do you think you're going?'

Sally stood on the veranda, hands on her hips. Her eyes followed Ray as she led Rain from the barn.

'I just need to go into town, Sally and get my stuff from the Sheriff. And I want to check on my place for myself.'

'Ray, you don't need to be riding out there by yourself now, you hear. Pete can get your things for you. He's been out your place every day fixing it up for you.'

Sally's brow creased, her arms folded tight.

'There's no way you'll get back here before it gets dark. Besides, you're just not mended right yet.'

Her tone switched abruptly from a demand to a plea.

'Please Ray, come back inside.'

'Really,' said Ray, 'I'll be fine. I can sleep out at my place tonight and head back here tomorrow.'

She mounted Rain, wincing as she settled into the saddle. Turning she gave Sally what she hoped was a reassuring smile.

'Sally, I appreciate your concern, really, but I'll be fine. I'll be seeing you tomorrow.'

She flicked her reins and nudged Rain into a walk. As she reached the ranch gates, she looked back. Sally was no longer there.

Ray reined her horse to a halt outside the Sheriff's office. She looked down at Bo and Jim, sitting out front sipping coffee and smoking cigarettes. As she slid from Rain's back, Jim flicked his cigarette butt over the railing and headed into the Sheriff's office. By the time Rain was hitched up, Sheriff Boone was there.

'Ray, it sure is good to see you up and about, although it looks to me like you're still on the road to recovery.'

His deep, smooth voice and well-meant words did nothing to ease Ray's agitation. She met the Sheriff's eye. He gestured to the seat Jim had just vacated.

'Sit yourself down girl, before you fall over. You're as pale as a ghost. I expect the ride out here took it out of you.'

He sent Bo inside and occupied his chair. Leaning forward he scrutinised Ray's bruised features.

'So what brings you here?'

'Come to get my belongings, and I wanted to take a look at those men that attacked me. They still here?'

Sheriff Boone nodded slowly.

'I see,' he said, 'you had second thoughts 'bout letting them be on their way?'

Ray twitched in her seat. She wasn't sure how she felt. She wanted to open her mouth and just let her words escape. But they were still churning around inside her, all tangled up with feelings. She made fists, forcing her nails to cut into her palms. Her breath audible, like the creak of the chair as she rocked back and forth.

The Sheriff saw the procession of emotions rippling across her face. She'd been through hell. He wasn't surprised to see her unravelling. He'd seen strong men go through a lot less and fall to pieces. And this woman wasn't put together right in the first place. He waited patiently for Ray to express herself.

'I jus' need to see them is all Sheriff. See them locked up. Put an end to what's goin' round my head. I don't want to wait 'n talk to the Marshall. So you can let them go in your own time. But I see their faces when I sleep. They're in my cabin, hurting me every night, and its eating me up inside. I can't let go Sheriff, and I can't make it stop. Maybe if I see them behind bars, they won't hurt me no more.'

The Sheriff nodded and rose from his chair.

'I guess that's a reasonable request you got there, Ray. I can't say how you're going to feel when you see them, but that's for you to deal with I'm afraid. Maybe you'll put your nightmares to bed, or maybe you'll make them worse, but that's your call.'

He held out a hand to help Ray up before walking slowly back into his office. Ray paused, took a deep breath and followed.

Jim and Bo were either side of a table, setting up for a game of cards. She looked past them, glimpsing the lock up. There were her attackers lounging on cots either side of the cell, one of them snoring gently. The Sheriff's spurs tinkled as he came up behind Ray. He extended an arm to stop her getting closer to the prisoners. One of the men opened his eyes and sat up. He squinted at Ray and the Sheriff. When he recognised her, a sly smile crossed his face. He reached out with his foot to nudge the other prisoner awake.

'Audley,' he said, eyes fixed on Ray, 'never guess who's come a visiting us.'

Audley removed his hat from his face. Rubbing his eyes, he levered himself into a sitting position. He took in the scene, and the brooding silence, before slowly standing and moving to the bars.

'Why, look at the little lady now, Cole. She looks fine and dandy to me. Seems like no actual harm came to her after all.'

He spoke quietly, his grating voice made the hairs on Ray's arms stand on end and her scalp tingle. Cole came up and stood next to his 'brother.'

'Why, she sure does look fine. Crazy as ever, but healthy.'

He barked out a laugh and turned to the Sheriff.

'Y'see, we didn't really do no harm to this witch. Sure we took a few little things from her place, ain't no way we can deny that. But the rest of it was self-defence. She tried to shoot us. Look at her now, all fixed up. Don't really seem like you need to be bothering the Marshall 'bout this now does it?'

Ray stared intently at her tormentors. She read their indifference, their scorn and disgust. Her life had no value. She was less than human in their eyes. The cell began to tilt; her knees turned to jelly. She desperately needed Earl. Needed his strength and calm comfort. Darkness invaded the corners of the lock up. Her eyelids fluttered, a long black tunnel was sucking her in. She reached out for support. And Earl was there to take her hand.

She took a deep shuddering breath and the room returned to sharp focus. She looked again at the men in the cell. Their dirt-brown, lined faces and dull eyes. Cruel, angry, uncaring creatures spending their lives taking from others then crawling away in the dark. Anger edged its way back in. These men had no right to hurt her in her own home. They had no right to take her belongings, to take her strength and her sureness, leaving nothing but pain and fear.

The silence dragged on. Ray's anger exulted her. Strength flooded through her body; pain and fear faded to nothing. Men like these bought nothing to the world. And she knew in that moment, the world would be better without them. She turned to the Sheriff, her voice emotionless.

'I'll take my stuff and go Sheriff. You can release them. They can't hurt me no more.'

Twenty-one

The Sheriff stood on the veranda watching Ray ride away; a frown creased his forehead.

She sat straight-backed in the saddle, gazing fixedly ahead, fuelled by anger and a sense of awful purpose. As Ray reached the edge of town, she reined in her mount, eyes slitted against the brightness of the sun. Rain fretted at the ground impatient for the freedom of the open country. Ray tipped her hat forward to shade her face and reached for her canteen. As she slaked her thirst she heard a gentle hum. Seconds later there was the familiar slap of Earl's moccasined feet on the hard-baked earth. The tension eased from her body. Smiling, she reached down and grabbed Earl's arm pulling him up behind her. She flicked the reins, urging Rain to a canter. Soon they were merging into the landscape, and the town was lost in their dust.

After a mile or so, Ray pulled Rain to a halt. She spoke quickly, quietly, still looking straight ahead.

'Earl, I know what I need to do,' she said.

He slid down and stood at Rain's head, looking up to Ray. The pony nuzzled his palm affectionately.

'Ray, I know what you intend doing, and I understand why, I really do. But you need to be prepared to face the consequences of your actions. D'you fully understand that?'

Ray looked down at Earl standing calmly in front of her. Within the fractured thoughts swirling in her head, there was one that rang clear and true. She'd punish the men that attacked her. They wouldn't hurt her or anyone else ever again. She needed to regain that part of her she lost that night — the part that could push back. The sentinel in her head, guarding against a world she'd never understood.

She reached out a hand to Earl.

'Please come with me. I know what I need to do. I don't have no choice. I'll take whatever comes my way from the doin' of it.'

Earl made no answer, just remounted behind her. Ray swung the reins pointing the pony toward the hills west of town. They reached a flat area, with boulders on one side, trees and scrub on the other. Remains of fires were scattered amongst the rocks. Branching from the main track a narrow pathway led into the hills. They dismounted and followed it up, picking their way through rocks and giant saguaro. Their route twisted round great outcrops taking them ever upwards. Ray looked down; the clearing was now well below them. The track turned again and their start point was lost to sight. After a while they reached a clearing surrounded by thorny shrubs, sheltered by a large overhang. Ray watered her horse and hitched him to a bush. Squeezing through the brush, they had a clear view of the main trackway below.

Earl pointed down there.

'If the deputies escort those cowboys out of town, they'll have to come this way. Reckon Jim and Bo will stop back there, at the main clearing, then head back to town. Expect your robbers will be heading for Timberland. It's a two-bit town far enough that no-one will know what's gone on here. I reckon they'll make camp for the night on the next patch of flat ground before heading off at first light. That's assuming the Sheriff lets them go today. If he waits till morning, they'll head straight on out, but they'll still have to take this pass.'

Ray unsaddled Rain and hefted a waterbag. She looked up; the sun was past midday, but it would be a long while before it got dark. Although it was hot and bright down on the plain, she felt the cool of the shade under their rocky outcrop. She went to gather kindling; Earl shook his head.

'Not a good idea to light a fire Ray, it'll give us away.' Ray laughed. There was a wry edge to her voice as she spoke.

'Good thought Earl. Imagine those boy's surprise if they come early and find us here.'

'Best settle up here nice and quiet. We'll catch them when they ride through. Today or tomorrow, what's the difference. Sound travels in these hills, we'll hear them coming one way or another.'

Ray and Earl lay quietly watching the sky, as the sun made its slow descent to the horizon. She was mesmerized by a single cloud scudding across the purple sky, highlighted by the setting sun.

There was a stillness in the air, and the plaintiff *caaaw* of a bird echoed eerily around her. The air was fresh and getting colder; she felt goosebumps rising on her skin. The ground began to release the heat of the day's sun and pain was creeping back in. She'd need to move, get her blood circulating. She went to rise, and felt Earl's warm hand grip hers. He shook his head, finger to his lips, sshhhh.

Ray froze. She lay still, straining her ears. But there was nothing but her own heartbeat and her own blood flowing ever faster. She forced herself to slow her breath. In the far distance she thought she heard the sounds of horses picking their way along the rocky path in the dimming light. She turned to Earl, eyes wide.

Is that them?

Once again Earl put his finger to his lips.

'Stay here,' he whispered.

He crawled to the edge of their camp. Peering over the scrub he recognised the two men riding slowly below.

They were slumped in their saddles, rocking to the motions of their mounts; one spoke, his voice rasping through the silence.

'Audley, we need to be camping about now. It's nigh on dark and I can't see a fucking thing.'

'Sure', Audley said, keeping a sharp eye on the path. 'Once this trail opens out a bit we'll make camp. No point risking going further when we can't see nothing.'

Earl watched them ride past, then crept back to Ray. She lay where he'd left her. Eyes tight shut, she'd slowed her breathing, focusing on the sounds of the landscape: her pony's restless shuffling, dry leaves rustling in the breeze, tiny scratchings of unknown desert creatures, a bird call far out on the distant plains. She kept her breathing slow and rhythmic losing grip of time. The last rays of the sun were dipping below the horizon. It was going to be a clear cold night. The moon stood loud and bright in the sky casting a silver shadow across the land.

She felt Earl's warmth and opened her eyes. He was crouching in front of her. He beckoned Ray to follow him. She reached for the rifle and checked the gun in her holster. Earl lead her silently towards Cole and Audley's camp.

He slowed, raising his hand, pointing to a large boulder; they dropped to a crouch and inched forward. Peering over the rock, Ray caught sight of Cole and Audley asleep by their saddles. Their horses hitched to a dead tree. They'd not made a fire just untacked their mounts and gone to sleep. Ray pumped her lungs full of oxygen. The cool night air did nothing to ease her rage. Without even glancing at Earl she strode towards the sleepers.

Audley jerked awake to the noise of her boots treading dirt. He scrambled to his knees reaching for his pistol. This roused Cole sending him toward his own gun. They froze at the sight of this tall, imposing figure levelling a Winchester at them.

Audley was first to find his voice.

'Who the hell are you? What do you want?' he whined. 'If you're looking for money you're plain out of luck. We got less than nothing.'

'Well, would you believe that,' said Ray scornfully. 'They don't even recognise me.'

She tipped back her hat, the moonlight illuminated her face.

'D'you recognise me, now?'

'What the fuck!' said Cole, glancing at Audley.

'You got one rifle bitch,' said Audley. 'At best, you can only hit one of us. Time you've done that one of us'll put a bullet in your gut. Telling you now, you shoot my brother, you'll be beggin' for death afore I finish with you.'

Ray glimpsed Earl, poised behind Cole. She jerked her head in Audley's direction, nodding. Cole threw a questioning look to Audley.

Did she have someone with her?

He looked behind them — not a soul there. He felt Audley next to him, tensing. His hand by his gun, ready to draw. No way would Audley be intimidated by this woman. He'll gut shoot her and then pluck out those fucking eyes while she was about the business of dyin'. Those pale, crazy eyes. He remembered those eyes when he was kicking the shit out of. They just stared at him the whole time, like she didn't care 'bout she was being beaten to death. Hell, that was the reason he kept on at her, he just wanted her to close her fucking eyes.

A shot rang out. Audley's head exploded. Cole felt his brother's hot blood splatter him, fragments of bone piercing his skin. The sound echoed around the landscape. He went for his gun. But it wouldn't leave the holster. Ray turned slowly and deliberately in his direction, smiling as she pulled the trigger.

Twenty-two

Dwain settled his horse in the barn and walked toward the cabin. He'd had a long day out on the range and was hungry and tired. He wanted nothing more than a bowl of Ma's stew, a cup of strong coffee, and a gut full of whiskey. He hadn't gone far, when he saw Sally standing on the veranda. When she spoke her voice was shrill with tension.

'Dwain, its Ray. She rode off this morning. I'm so worried.'

'Hold on Ma, can we just go inside and talk about this, while I get myself something to eat and drink?'

'Dwain, listen to me. She rode off. Said she'd be going to the Sheriff's office to get her things. Then she'd check on her place, sleep out there tonight. But I'm worried. I don't think she's strong enough yet. I know you won't want to, but I need someone to head on out there and check on her.'

Dwain stared at her. He could care less if Ray'd ridden out. Opposite was true. He was pretty happy about it. He hated her being in the cabin. He hated the intensity in her eyes when she looked at him; he couldn't fathom what was going on in her head. He could feel her presence all the time, even when she was hidden away in Ma's room. The very air in the cabin thickened, became poisoned with her. He spent as little time there as possible. He took a deep breath before responding, trying to keep his voice calm and steady.

'Look Ma, if she's well enough to get on her horse and ride out, then I don't know what you're worrying about. Maybe it's time.'

Dwain and Sally turned their heads in unison as they heard Pete's horse approach.

'There you go Ma, get Pete to go look for you. He'll be as worried about her as you.'

Pete dismounted and walked toward them.

'What's up, something wrong?'

'Ma's worried, 'cos Ray took her horse and rode out...'
Sally interrupted.
She told Pete what had happened.
'She knew she wouldn't get back here before dark. Said she'd sleep at her place. She ain't healed yet. Anything could happen.'
Pete could hardly miss the smug look on his brother's face.
'OK Ma,' he said kindly, 'let me grab some water and grub and I'll ride on over there.'
He scanned the sky.
'No chance I'll be back before daybreak. Don't want to risk my horse breaking a leg out there in the dark.'
Sally shot Pete a relieved smile before heading into the cabin to fetch supplies for the trail. Dwain shook his head and wished Pete a safe ride. Pete watched his brother stride into the cabin, doubting his sincerity. While later Sally emerged with a canteen of water and a parcel of food.
'Here you go, son. Just some biscuits and bacon, but it'll see you through the night. There's enough for Ray too, she didn't take nothing with her.'
'Thanks, Ma. Don't worry 'bout me. Be back in the morning, with Ray safe and sound.'
Sally watched her son ride off, as the sky darkened. She could already see a pink blush on the horizon. It wouldn't be long before sunset. She clasped her hands tight fighting the tension in her body. Now she'd another to worry about.
Of her sons, Pete had always been her favourite. She knew it was wrong to prefer one boy over the other, but Pete had always had a kindly temperament. Dwain was cut from the same cloth as his Pa. He had a wicked temper and he could be a hard man. She knew that Dwain would make the ranch work now he was in charge, and he'd take care of her and Pete. But she knew she wouldn't always like the way he did it.

Pete rode steadily letting his horse pick her own way. She walked, her stride long and steady, with her head hung low as if she were checking the path ahead.
The sun was approaching the horizon. It wouldn't be long before it was dark. Night fell quick out on the plains. Pete knew men who'd pushed their horses too hard in the dark and been dead

in the dirt next day.

By the time Pete reached the turn in the track leading to Ray's place the night was black as molasses. The moon was just off new, giving pitiful little light. But it was a cloudless night and his horse could see well enough. No chance he'd be able to see to follow Ray's trail though. Pete paused at the junction before turning his horse and heading in the direction of Ray's place. It wasn't long before he caught sight of the farmstead.

'Hey there Ray!' he yelled. 'It's Pete.'

He didn't want to spook Ray and be hit by a bullet for his troubles. But as he got closer to the cabin, he knew Ray wasn't there. There was no smoke from the fire, or candlelight seeping out through the shutters. He led his horse to the barn and, as he expected, it was empty. He untacked and watered his horse, and put her in a stall for the night. He was hauling his saddle bags and rifle to the cabin, when he heard a gunshot.

He'd ducked before he realised the bullet wasn't intended for him. Holding his breath, he listened intently. The shot didn't sound close and he couldn't place the direction. Another shot rang out. Maybe some cowboys out hunting their dinner. But no harm in getting inside and behind the now fixed up door.

Pete raked out the grate and set a fire. Then he drew up a chair in front of the hearth and heated his dinner. He kept his holster on and his rifle propped next to him whilst he ate sizzling bacon and warm bread. Whilst he watched the shadow shapes created by the flickering flames, he wondered where Ray was at. He couldn't have crossed with her on his way into the homestead. If she'd been on her way back from town he'd have seen her. He knew she was tough and she'd get over her physical injuries, but he was worried about her. A beating could do strange things to a person, and Ray wasn't quite like other folk to start with. He hadn't seen much of her since he'd brought her back to the ranch, she spent most of her time in Ma's room. The first time he'd seen her with her head shaved was when the Sheriff came to call, and he'd been shocked. She was thin and gaunt, almost skeletal. When he'd looked into her eyes, he couldn't see the Ray he'd known as a girl. He was sure she was still in there, but there was something else too, something different. But as strange as she looked, he still felt an urge to take care of her, to look after her. He'd rest and ride out in the morning and look for some sign as to where she'd gone.

Pete awoke with a start. The fire was still burning and he was slumped in the chair, his hat had fallen onto the floor next to him. He sat upright and listened. A few seconds later, he heard a murmuring that he was sure was coming from outside. He reached slowly for his rifle . There it was again, murmuring and whispering. Pete crept to the window. Flattening himself against the wall, he craned his neck to peer through the shutters.

The night was clear, and the sky was filled with stars, the moon bright in the sky. The scene outside was like a tapestry woven in black and white thread. He couldn't see anything that would cause such a noise. He crouched low, creeping under the window. He checked the view from the other side, craning his neck. He took a sharp breath. There was a man with a rifle standing with his back to the outside wall of the cabin. Pete reasoned he must have been attracted by the smoke from the chimney, or the firelight through the window.

The figure moved closer to the door. Pete eased open the shutter and took aim at the man.

'Hold up,' he yelled, 'you sneakin' about outside. There's my Winchester pointed at you right now. Step away from the cabin with your hands in the air.'

Pete waited for a response. All he heard was whispering and murmuring, like people quietly cursing in a language he didn't understand. He strained his eyes through the shadows to see if there was anyone else around. Hell, for all he knew there as a whole gang of them. He called out again.

'Last chance mister. Step out with your hands up or I'm going to put a bullet in you.'

There came a voice. Soft but clear in the quiet night air.

'So, you're going to shoot me from my own cabin, then?'

'Ray, is that you? It's me, Pete.'

'Well, Pete, I'm going to come inside my cabin, and I don't want you shooting me. Then you'll kindly explain why you're in my place, pointing a gun at me.'

Pete stepped away from the window. He should have been relieved, but his rifle stayed trained on the door. He heard footsteps approaching and Ray's voice, muttering. The door creaked open slowly, and Ray stepped into the cabin. Pete glanced behind her, expecting someone else, but Ray was alone. He scanned her features in the firelight. Even up close, she could be mistaken for a man. Tall and thin, with a stubbled head, a holster on one hip and her rifle held loosely in her hand. Her limbs moved awkwardly, stiff like a marionette. She took off her hat, and gave Pete a toothy grin that barely reached her unreadable eyes.

'Do you want to explain why you're in my cabin?'

'Ma was worried about you. Sent me to find you. See if you was OK. That's all. Perhaps you might tell me where you've been?' She looked past Pete and shook her head.

'Went into town like I told your Ma. Saw the Sheriff and got my stuff. See?' She held up her Pa's rifle. 'I'm pretty tired now, all I want is my bed. You can stay here and sleep if you want.'

With that Ray shuffled through to the back room and shut the door. Pete shivered. Despite the fire, the cabin was suddenly cold. He stoked the embers and tossed on another log. Returning to the chair He held his rifle across his knees, pointing toward the door. His eyes began to close. He couldn't put his finger on it. Ray was unharmed; why didn't he feel relieved? Something wasn't right.

He'd set his mind to figuring out what in the morning.

Twenty-three

When Pete woke, the sun was beginning its climb into the sky and the fire was cold and dead in the grate. His stomach rumbled and he ate a biscuit he'd saved from last night's dinner. He poked around in Ray's cabin and managed to find a bag of coffee he'd left from the last time he was out fixing things up. He sure as hell needed a cup. He re-lit the fire and put a pot of coffee on to heat up. He'd heard nothing from Ray's room. While the coffee was heating, he took a walk outside to the barn. There was Ray's horse in the stall next to his. He'd half expected to see a third horse. He shook his head; Ray must have been talking to herself. Maybe Dwain was right, the girl was getting crazier by the day.

When Pete stepped back into the cabin Ray was pouring herself coffee.

'See you're up girl. You want to tell me what you was doin' last night, 'cos you sure was back late for just a trip to town?'

Ray carried on looking out of the window.

'Told you, Pete. Went into town to collect up my stuff. Took me a while. Guess I'm not healed right yet. I rode pretty slow is all.'

She turned to Pete, beaming a shy smile. This time Pete felt it was genuine. Her eyes looked softer and little clearer.

'Thank you for fixing up my place. Think I'm about ready to move back in. Just need to take stock of what's here and fill up on supplies. Guess I'm mighty lucky Sheriff Boone was able to get my money back.'

Pete thought carefully before he spoke. 'Maybe, you and I can ride back to the ranch together this morning, after we take stock of what's here. I'm not sure you're well enough to be riding too far. We could take the wagon into town tomorrow for supplies. Ma sure would be happy to see you're safe.'

'Oh, I'm fine for riding, so long as I take it slow and steady. Sure, I'm still hurting, but I'm getting better every day. Maybe, you could go back and see your Ma for me? Tell her I'm OK.'

'I don't know, Ray. I think Ma deserves to see you after what she's done for you. We can ride together. You still got some explaining to do about what you was doing last night.'

He held up his hand to forestall interruption.

'Yeah, I know, you're still hurting and you rode slow. But that still don't explain why you was back here so late. Unless you was sitting in Pete Wallace's saloon half the night?' Pete paused and looked intently at Ray. 'There were gunshots last night, I heard them after I arrived here. You hear anything, or know something about that?'

Ray heard Earl's voice.

'You can't tell him what you did. He'll have to tell the Sheriff. He'll tell them all, Sally, his brother. They'll call you a murderer.

Ray closed her eyes, shutting out the world.

'But I just took my life back. They were just going to ride away like nothing happened. Everyone thinks I'm crazy. The Marshall wouldn't have done nothing; the Sheriff just wanted them out of town. No. I had to stand up to them, make them pay for what they did to me.

'I know Ray,' said Earl, 'I'm on your side. But you need to keep it all to yourself. Just let them see one side of you, girl. No one needs to know. Ride back to the ranch with Pete. Go see Sally. They'll look out for you.'

Pete stared, wondering if he should do something.

Ray stood still as a statue, lips moving, like she was conducting a whispered conversation. Suddenly she opened her eyes, blinking back to this time and place.

'No Pete,' she said, like nothing had happened, 'I don't know nothing about no gunshots. Maybe you're right about heading back to the ranch — let's ride.'

Pete and Ray arrived back at the Mickleton place. There was a buggy parked up and horses hitched to the rail. Men stood on the veranda, talking with Sally and Dwain. Closer, Ray recognised Sheriff Boone, Deputy Jim and the Doc. They turned as Ray and Pete came into view.

Pete dismounted and took the reins from Ray, hitching their horses to the rail. Together they walked up the steps onto the veranda to questioning looks from those gathered. Sally made to speak, but a look from the Sheriff silenced her and she took a step back, hands wringing her apron. She looked relieved at seeing them safe. But there was something else in the glance she gave the lawmen.

Sheriff Boone stepped towards Ray and Pete. His tall frame cast a long shadow across the sun-bleached planks of the veranda. He tipped his hat back on his head.

'Guess we're all mighty glad to see you two safe.'

He turned his gaze to Ray.

'And it sure looks like you're making a recovery girl. I know the Doc here would very much like to take a look at you. He was sure surprised when I told him you're up and riding. Before that, perhaps you could tell me where you two were at last night.'

Behind the Sheriff's shoulder Ma stood rigid, concern etched on her face. Next to her Dwain looked fit to explode. Pete met the Sheriff's eye. He was about to reply when Ray jumped in.

'After I left town, I went to my cabin to see what state it had been left in. I want to move back soon as I can. Anyhow, Pete stopped by to check I was doin' OK after my ride to town. It was too late to ride back here so we stayed the night by the fire.'

Pete was confused, what the hell was going on?

He shrugged.

'Sure that's it. Ma was worried after Ray rode off. She sent me out to her place to check on her. We spent the night there, just like Ray says.'

Dwain shuffled from foot to foot, glaring at Ray. Pete looked back at the Sheriff.

'What's going on? Why are you so concerned where Ray and me spent the night? You're a sheriff not a preacher.'

'Well son, Jim and Bo rode Audley and Cole out to the hill pass late yesterday afternoon, make sure they went on their way and bothered no other folk.'

He paused and turned to Ray.

'They were found on the trail this morning with bullets in their heads.'

Pete's heart skipped a beat. He resisted the urge to turn to Ray. Those gunshots he'd heard last night before Ray turned up with all that insane whispering. How long after the shots he couldn't tell because he'd fallen asleep.

Ray shrugged.

'Can't say I'm all broke up over that news. But I don't know why y'all looking at me. I was out at my place. Isn't that right, Pete?'

Pete felt everyone's eyes on him.

'That's right. I got there just after dark, lit a fire and ate some food Ma gave me and slept the night. It's not such a good idea to be riding in the dark, and I'm mighty glad we weren't, seeing as how there was gunman out there.'

'Think carefully on it Pete, said the Sheriff. Did you see anyone else out riding when you was heading over to the Crow place?'

'No Sheriff, Didn't see nobody.'

Jim took a step forward.

'What about gunshots Pete? Did you hear anything?'

Ray jumped in.

'We didn't hear nothing,' she turned to Pete, 'did we Pete?'

'No, we didn't hear nothing.'

'Well that's pretty strange ain't it?' said Jim, 'cos they was definitely shot last night. They was alive when I left them, and they was found dead this morning. Your place ain't too far away Ray, and the sound of those gunshots would have carried for miles. You sure you didn't hear nothing?'

Ray turned a hard face on the Deputy.

'Jim, I said we didn't hear nothing, and we didn't see nothing neither. Hell, maybe you shot them, just rode them out of town and put a bullet in them? Anyone ever think on that, maybe check his gun.'

Sheriff Boone took a step in front of Jim.

'That's enough, folks. I won't have accusations like that thrown around. We came out here to see if anyone knew anything. And, you have to admit, it's natural we might be asking questions, considering what those boys did to you, Ray. But we'll leave things as they are for now. Ray, perhaps you might like to step inside with Sally and the Doc. He'd sure like to check you out, make sure that you're healing fine.'

The Sheriff turned to the Doc.

'I'll be heading back into town now, but I'll leave Jim here with you so you can ride back into town together, case there's murderers still around. Let me know how Ray's doing when you get time.'

Sally followed Ray and the Doc inside.

The Sheriff went to untie his horse from the rail. He felt tension building between Dwain and Pete. Pete was calm as a prairie breeze, and Dwain looked like he'd a twister brewing. The Sheriff was professionally curious, happy to wait and see what came out. Something was going on here. He was determined to find out what.

Twenty-four

The Doc made his way up the stairs onto the veranda, and then through the door into the Sheriff's office. His haste caused him to puff a little, and his eagerness added weight to his footfall. Sheriff Boone and his deputies were discussing the deaths of Audley and Cole, when they heard his arrival. They paused their deliberations; the Sheriff smiled a greeting.

'How can we help you, Doc?'

'Came by to be letting you know I've given Ray Crow a clean bill of health. Point of fact, she's doing a helluva lot better than I'd been expecting. Safe to say the girl is on the mend.' He took in a couple more deep breaths, looking for a chair.

'Here,' said the Sheriff, dragging his own chair from behind his desk. 'Take a seat there. You look like you need it more'n me.'

The Doc held up a hand in thanks.

'I sure do,' he said, sitting, easing down a body creaking as much as the chair that suffered his bulk. 'Did I hear you boys talking about them killings up in the pass? There ain't no-one going to miss them fellas, that's for sure. Are you going to let it ride Sheriff, or are you still chasing down a suspect?'

'You're right Doc. Folk can sure sleep easier in their beds now. But we can't forget that someone committed murder. Them boys were shot in cold blood. And that killer is likely living with us, here in town or thereabouts. I ain't settling for that. How can I?'

Deputy Bo took a step forward, squared his shoulders and addressed the Doc directly.

'We've been thinking, it's most likely Pete Mickleton that did it. Unless there was someone else out there we didn't know about with a grudge against those two. They didn't have nothing to steal, and they was heading on out of town.'

'Now Bo, it might not be a good idea to be pointing fingers quite so openly.' said the Sheriff with a disapproving glance.

'Perhaps you might like to busy yourself making us a pot of coffee. Doc, will you stay a while for a cup? You look mighty comfortable in my chair.'

'Indeed I will. I could sure rest my bones a little longer.'

Later, coffee in hand, the Doc turned his attention back to the Sheriff.

'Are you really considering young Pete? I'm not sure that boy has it in him to squash a bug, let alone commit murder. His brother on the other hand, I'm sure he's likely capable, but for the life of me, I can't see him having a reason.'

The Sheriff shrugged.

'Short of the murders being done by some ornery passing stranger, only person with motive and opportunity has to be young Pete Mickleton.'

'Well Sheriff that ain't exactly true,' said Jim. 'I know you don't think she's capable, but Ray Crow sure had a pressing reason.'

Before the Sheriff could reply, the Doc spoke up.

'Agree with you there Jim. Ray sure would be motivated. But given the beating she took she wouldn't be capable. Even if she could make it up there, she ain't got what it takes to kill someone. Not saying she's fully right in the head, but she's no killer.'

Bo glanced at Jim. Bo said what they were thinking.

'What if they was in it together? Maybe she wanted those cowboys killed and Pete did it for her?'

'Well son,' said the Sheriff, 'maybe you got yourself a point there. I've been upholding the law for a long time now, and folks just keep on doing things you don't expect them to. Things they don't seem capable of. I ain't going to count nothing, or nobody, out. But right now, we got no evidence and no witnesses. We got nothing but a whole lot of speculation. Till we got something I can hang my hat on I guess we just carry on keeping this town safe and orderly.'

'Anyhow,' said the Doc, 'I got me some more to say on the subject of Ray Crow. After I'd done examining Ray, Sally approached me, and, well, the long and the tall of it is, Sally thinks Ray is her daughter.'

Silence.

All eyes on the Doc.

'Afore your time Sheriff, but you might have caught rumours.

Some twenty years ago Sally Mickleton was set upon by a couple of passing bounty hunters. Jared Mickleton came home from town one day to find Sally unconscious and in bad shape out front, and the oldest boy Dwain sitting out there on the dirt next to her. Anyhow, Jared fixed her up best he could. Some say, he went after those fellas and shot 'em both dead.

Anyhow, Sally recovered from the attack, but it wasn't long before it was clear she was with child. Jared, well he was mad as hell. I'm told he took that anger out on Sally. And those two boys, 'specially Dwain, bore the brunt of it. But that baby held on in there. When the time came, Jared called out Lena Crow. Now Lena and her husband Melvin hadn't been in the homestead long. They'd come out on a train from Oregon. Everyone knew that Lena had a way with the herbs, and she knew about birthing. So old man Mickleton got her out to the ranch, and she saw Sally through the birth, but that baby was born dead, so I'm told. Now to this day, Sally's never been off that spread and no one would say a word about things to Jared, less they wanted to be on the wrong side of his fist, or his gun.'

The Sheriff began to pace.

'So Doc, all that is mighty interesting, but why does Sally think Ray's her daughter?'

'Thing is, when they first came out this way no-one knew that Lena and Melvin Crow had a child. Lena didn't come into town much and Melvin came in for the store and the saloon. He liked to drink, gamble and sometimes whore, if he had enough money. But he didn't have no friends, and he didn't talk much. Then a couple of years after what happened with Sally, Melvin had some men over to his homestead to build his barn and they said there was a small child there, a girl. They said she was a strange looking creature. And she didn't look nothing like Lena or Melvin.'

'Doc, I ain't seeing no mystery here,' said the Sheriff. 'So Lena and Melvin kept to themselves and had a strange looking child. There ain't nothing too suspicious about that.'

The Doc sat back eyes moving from face to face. It was Jim spoke first.

'Let me get this straight Doc, Lena Crow helps Sally Mickleton to give birth, and the baby was birthed still. Then it seems Lena has a child, and now Sally thinks the child is hers. I don't get why she thinks that. Don't make no sense to me.'

'Well Jim,' said the Doc, 'here's the nub of it. When I spoke to Sally yesterday, she told me about the day she got attacked. One of the men that... you know, was a peculiar looking fella. Tall and skinny and bald, with the whitest skin she'd ever saw and these watery blue eyes. Says they looked like the Devil's eyes. An' when Ray was dressed in Jared's clothes, head all shaved, it was like she saw a ghost.'

The Sheriff paused his pacing.

'Holy shit Doc, you sure left the best till last. Maybe you should give up on medicine and be telling stories in a travelling show. OK, answer me this. Does Dwain know anything about the attack on his Ma and her being with child?'

'Like I said, he was only young, barely five. No one knows if he saw what happened. No one asked him, not even Jared. And from what Sally told me, when Lena came to see to the birthing Jared took the boys off the ranch.'

No one spoke.

The Sheriff perched on the edge of his desk. He crossed his arms, a wry smile creasing his face.

'Well I'll be dammed. Wouldn't take much of a spark to set off that powder keg.'

Twenty-five

From the veranda, Sally watched Ray and Pete ride away, heading back to Ray's place. Ray was riding Rain, Pete following behind with the wagon. Ray sat tall on her horse, her back straight, her hat tipped forward shielding her face from the sun.

Sally wasn't convinced Ray was fully recovered. There was a strangeness to the way she moved, like her joints weren't right. And there was that haunted look on her face. Sally thought she may still be in a lot of pain, but Ray never complained. Wasn't so much the physical injuries worried Sally, more the state of her mind. She seemed in a world of her own, like she was living in two places at once. Sally knew, better than most what suffering does to a person. It changed you inside. Left you vulnerable and awkward, not knowing your place in creation. Sally felt Ray had left herself behind somehow, someplace, and wondered if she would ever find her way back.

As they reached the gates of the ranch, Ray turned and looked at Sally, tipping her hat and nodding a grateful goodbye. Sally could feel the power in those pale eyes of hers and felt a chill. Ray's presence unearthed memories she'd spent years burying. The nightmares were back, panic threatened to break free any moment. She waved and turned back to the cabin. If she was honest, she felt relieved to see the back of Ray, despite her concerns for her. Maybe with her gone things would settle on the ranch, then she and her boys could focus on the future.

Sally set to preparing the evening meal. Dwain was out working; the ranch house was quiet, leaving space for her mind to wander.

She recalled confiding in the Doc yesterday, worried about what she might've stirred up.

What if he told anyone in town? What if it got back to Dwain or Pete?

Nevertheless, it was a relief to get it off her chest. On the other hand, saying it out loud made it real, and the events of twenty years ago seemed like yesterday. She remembered when Lena had rushed to the ranch to help her. She'd watched her husband, and children ride off into town knowing the consequences if Lena couldn't fix the problem. Her husband had made it clear that if she had the baby, he would kill it. The pregnancy had already nearly destroyed her family.

She was worried about Pete too. He'd reassured her he'd no intentions toward Ray. He felt sorry for her was all. Sally forced herself to believe him. He'd always been a kind boy, so different from his father and his brother. Maybe he was telling the truth. But she went back to when he was a boy and he'd taken to visiting the Crow place. He always had another reason, but she'd been convinced it was because of the Crow girl. But then one day, he'd stopped going. He'd never said why and she'd never asked.

Now she was wondering what had happened. She shook her head, riddled with misgivings

Too much time thinking don't do a person no good, makes you want things you can't have, change things you can't undo.

Her own Ma had always said that hard work and prayer were the only ways to keep your feet on the ground. She hadn't prayed for the longest time. Not since those bounty hunters turned up at the ranch. She paused, then shook her head, taking in a long deep breath.

No, she wasn't about to start along those lines again.

When Pete returned from Ray's, Dwain had finished work, a stew was ready on the stove, and the ranch house was tidy and swept. As she served dinner, she felt a peace settle on her. The boys were more relaxed than they'd been in weeks. They even exchanged a joke over the meal. After they'd finished they headed outside to enjoy a whiskey on the veranda. Ray's presence seemed like a distant memory. She felt sure things would turn out just fine. They'd get through this drought as a family. Life would get back to normal.

Twenty-six

Pete was on his way to Ray's place. He'd been in town collecting supplies for the ranch. Whilst he was there, he'd picked up things for Ray as well. He'd been riding out to her place regularly, finishing fixing the cabin, repairing the barn. Winter would soon be upon them. He needed to get the cabin secure and stack a couple of cords of wood for the fire. There was no saving her crops; the drought had done for them; they'd been left to rot back into the ground. He and Dwain put more of their cattle onto Ray's land to keep them fed. They'd agreed to pay Ray something for the grazing. That meant she could buy enough food to survive through winter. Hopefully the drought would break, and she could plant again next season. Dwain wasn't happy with the arrangement but couldn't argue against it.

Ma seemed happy to see the back of Ray. She'd cared for her day and night with a dedication the brothers had rarely seen. But once Ray was up and about she didn't want to be near her. Pete thought Ma seemed a little scared of Ray. Now even he was beginning to think that she might be a little crazy. She'd always been different. But there was a softness to her, and a lightness that lifted her up a little from the drudgery of frontier life. Her recent behaviour could be downright odd at times. He sensed a hardness that wasn't there before. No doubt the legacy of the beating she took. Blows to the head could do that to a person. He'd seen it with cowhands kicked by a horse. She talked a lot to herself these days, adding to the oddity of her general behaviour. He'd often seen her whispering when she thought she was alone. It had shocked him at first, but he thought little of it now.

Ray's bruises had long since faded. Her hair was growing back bright red and lustrous. Although it was still short it neatly framed her face, highlighting her strong features. Pete thought she was beautiful. He remembered when he'd first seen her. A willowy girl with white skin and mesmerising blue eyes. She was different now, more angled, tougher, but still beautiful. He felt drawn to this new Ray in ways that excited and terrified him.

Pete was loading supplies into the barn when Ray appeared in the doorway. She'd taken to dressing like a man all the time now with trousers, boots and a holstered gun. She even wore the hat that used to be his Pa's. She leaned against the door frame and smiled at him.

'Took your time, didn't you.' Pete smiled back.

'Well girl, I was doing your chores, so I decided to take my payment by drinking a whiskey in the saloon. Seemed like you owed me that.'

Ray laughed and the sound of it made Pete's stomach flip, as he watched her turn and walk away. She reappeared a few seconds later with a sack of oats, nudging Pete as she pushed past him. He noticed the smile still on her face and he couldn't help but smile back. The two of them finished unloading the wagon in a companionable silence. Although the days were cooler how, after the ride from town, and unloading supplies, Pete could feel sweat and dust coating his face. He walked outside to dunk his head into a bucket of water, washing off the grime.

Pete returned to the barn, shaking off his wet hair. Ray was leaning against her horse's flank, whispering to him, stroking his neck, calm and relaxed. Pete felt a stabbing pang of attraction. Taking her hand, he led her away from the horse. He removed his Pa's old hat from her head, so he could better see her face. Her eyes were the palest blue he'd ever seen. Forget what others said, she was beautiful.

But there was something else. Something he couldn't read. Like only part of Ray was ever present. He stroked her short hair. Her expression didn't change. Bending his head forward he kissed her lips. When he pulled back, her eyes were blank, her gaze distant.

Did she want him to continue or not?

He kissed her again, harder this time. Ray remained unmoved, but for a slight smile on her lips, which didn't extend much further. It was like her mind was elsewhere. Pete knew this was wrong, he should leave, but he couldn't make himself go. Through this confusion of emotions he was certain of one thing. He wanted Ray.

She's not objecting is she?

He kissed her again and this time he didn't hold back, letting desire overtake him. He was hard now. A tidal wave of feelings flowed over him: desire, excitement, anger and shame. He couldn't stop — he was doing this.

Ray felt Pete's hands on her body. His lips on her lips. She didn't truly understand what was happening. She didn't know what to feel, or how to respond.

Squeezing her eyes tight shut, she felt panic rising and the beginnings of despair. But then Earl materialised from the shadows, his hand reaching for hers. As ever, Earl was there to save her, comfort her. He was her dark angel, and as she watched, his black, lustrous wings appeared from his back. His top hat softening into a plume of iridescent feathers. That great beak appearing between those glittering sharp black eyes. And the red and gold trimmed waistcoat shimmering into a coat of fine feathers. As their hands touched, she felt the draft from Earl's wings as he began to pull her upwards. Her own wings began to unfurl and together they took to the air, wheeling and swooping, calling to each other. Teasing the wind with their wings.

Ray caught a glimpse of the barn below, set in a barren rainless landscape. Snared by curiosity, she circled lower. Her sharp eyes penetrating the cracks in the roof. And there she was, pale, featherless and vulnerable amidst the piles of hay. Pete was pinning her down, his movements synchronising with the beat of her wings. To her astonishment she realised her body was responding. Unsure what to think, she soared away until she no longer felt connected with events below. She stayed in the air until exhausted, and her eyes began to close. Her wings were becoming smaller, soon they were gone completely. Earl caught her as she tumbled through the air. Together they descended to the floor of the barn.

She blinked open her eyes to Pete shaking her, looking down with concern.

He dressed, giving her a sad smile.

'Get dressed now, Ray,' he said. 'I've got chores back at the ranch. I'll come out to see you tomorrow if nothing else ain't pressing.'

Ray leaned against the doorway in numb silence as Pete climbed aboard his rig and flicked the reins. There she stayed until he was but a dust spec in the distance. Moisture rimming her eyes, as she followed the path of a black feather floating down from the hayloft.

Pete reined in his horse. He was halfway between the Mickleton ranch and Ray's homestead. Yesterday he'd told her he'd return, now he wasn't sure he should. He thought about what happened in the barn, what he'd done. The feelings were so strong for her. But afterwards there came a wave of shame. Yes, Ray's body had responded, but he knew that her mind had been elsewhere. He'd taken her body, but far from feeling satisfaction, he'd been left hollow inside.

He'd not seen many examples of kindness between man and woman. His Pa hadn't always been kind to his Ma. If Jared wanted her, he took her, like that was a husband's right. He'd hated his Pa for that, but hadn't he done the self-same thing? He'd never wanted to be like Jared, not in any way, not like this.

He urged his horse to walk on. He'd carry on and see Ray, and face her reaction, whatever it may be. She deserved that much.

When he reached the homestead, he found her out back preparing to burn off the dead crops.

'Hey there, farmer, what you up to?' Pete called, wary of her reaction. A smile lit up Ray's face.

'I'm going to do a burn. Pa used to do it at the end of the season. He reckoned it's good for the land and helps the crops grow better next year.'

'Can I help?'

'Sure, we got to dig a channel round the outside of the field, so the fire doesn't spread. Not that there's anything to catch, but that's the way you got to do it.'

Ray and Pete spent the next several hours digging channels on either sides of the field. Pete felt her companionship from afar seeking absolution in hard toil. From time to time he'd see Ray as she straightened. Sometimes she'd gesticulate in the air, talking as with an invisible presence. Her behaviour was child-like. It comforted him to see her relaxed and happy, even if she was acting a little crazy. He thought on the events of yesterday. He wasn't sure Ray understood what they'd done. Aware he'd taken advantage of her, he vowed it wouldn't happen again. He'd care for her, support her, but he'd never impose himself on her. His thoughts drifted back to that day, five years ago, when he'd kissed Ray the first time. Then came Melvin Crow bursting into the barn pointing his Winchester at him. Ray's Ma telling him, he wasn't welcome. Saying he couldn't be kissing her like that. He thought, maybe now, he understood why.

Work done, Ray and Pete collapsed. The earth was hard, and the shovel work backbreaking. Every inch of them was dirt brown. Sweat had run down their faces leaving meandering white streaks. Laughing at the state of themselves, they headed back to the cabin. Ray held the bucket whilst Pete cranked the pump handle. They drank their fill and Ray stripped off to wash. Pete tried not to stare as she doused her naked body with water. She seemed unconcerned to be naked in front of him. Pete could feel desire rising. He headed off to the barn, reappearing a while later with his horse.

'Be heading back to the ranch now Ray.'

'Sure Pete, thanks for your help today. Will you be by again soon?'

'I expect so Ray. Meantime, you take care now, you hear.'

Pete mounted his horse and rode back to the ranch. His body tired, his mind in turmoil.

Twenty-seven

Ray's life on the homestead had settled into a routine. The days shortened with the coming of winter, and the world seemed muted and quiet. Cold sunk its teeth into the land, suppressing the dust, changing the face of the landscape. From sun up to sun down Ray worked her land as best she could. She cleared scrub from around the cabin, fixed up holes in the barn to keep the winter out, and cared for her horse. She hunted when she needed and the weather permitted. Tracking game through the skeletal woods, her breath formed clouds in the air, and an eerie silence blanketed everything. She relied on Earl to seek out game. She felt an odd mix of sadness and excitement when she tracked an animal and finished it with a bullet. Sometimes, she was close enough that after the shot, she could watch the last of the life drain from the animal's eyes. Every time this happened her pulse quickened; power and energy flowing through her veins. Simultaneously, tears leaked from her eyes at the overwhelming finality of death.

Over the short winter months, Pete visited when he could to help her out. They would work together, draped in coats sown of animal furs, hats pulled down hard on their heads to keep out the cold. They laboured in companionable silence and then when the work was done, they would sit on the veranda, bundled in blankets, watching sun begin its descent. Pete would leave before darkness fell, then she would retreat into her cabin to sit in front of the fire, watching the flames warming the air. She remembered different times, when her and Ma would sit together, melting candle stubs and grinding herbs. Those days seemed so long ago. She felt like a different person now. Earl would join her in the cabin, and his company was a great comfort, easing her anxiety and her loneliness. Earl liked Pete. He said Pete cared for her and wanted to keep her safe. Earl's presence was strong when Pete was around. When the Doc came out to check on her, or the Sheriff, Earl's presence would be faint and his words so quiet she could barely hear them. But when Pete was around, they could talk and laugh. She felt safe with them both.

One thing that greatly troubled Ray was the nightmares. At night, when she slept, she would see horrible things. Cold eyes staring into hers, fists and boots raining blows on her. She saw bodies sleeping under blankets. One by one, she shot them dead. She waded through phantom lakes of blood to rip the covers from dead men's faces. Sometimes, she saw the bodies of Ma and Pa frozen under the earth. Other times, it was the man with the cold eyes, or Pete, and sometimes it was the body of a faceless child. Each time, she woke with tears burning her eyes. She would turn to Earl and he would hold her like a child. He'd rock her back and forth until she slept again or the sun came up.

Then one day, as Ray looked up at the sky, she saw nothing but blue as far as the eye could see. A cloudless panorama brightening everything beneath it. She felt a faint warmth in the air, and she could hear the faint *caaawing* of ravens in the sky. Her heart lifted at the sound that had been missing for the last few months. The sound that heralded the arrival of spring, that time of renewal and hope. She should soon be able to lay down crops for the coming year, but it still hadn't rained.

The springs were full of water. It travelled through the ground from those high mountains in the distance. The cold clear water had sustained Ray and Rain over the winter, but wouldn't satisfy a field of corn. She searched the sky again, hoping that clouds would appear over the horizon, but she saw nothing but blue. She reached up and felt her hair. It was getting long and she could feel it starting to matt again. She tried to wash and comb it, but mostly she forgot. It didn't feel important.

As she stood under the vast sky, Ray reached down and felt her belly. Over the last few weeks, she had felt something was wrong. She could feel a taut roundness and her body felt strange. She wondered whether she was ill, or she'd eaten something bad. She closed her eyes and enjoyed the feel of the warmth of the spring sun on her face. Ray smiled, as she heard footsteps behind her and turning, she saw Earl approaching. Then suddenly her belly rolled and pulsed as if it had been grasped from inside by invisible hands. She clutched at it and feeling her knees weaken, she collapsed onto the dirt, her mouth open with shock. In an instant, Earl was kneeling at her side.

'Ray, what's wrong?' he asked, his voice full of concern.

'I don't know, Earl, I'm scared.' Ray put her hand on Earl's shoulder and raised herself up to standing. She looked down at the mound of her belly. 'Something's wrong with me.'

Earl placed a hand on her belly. As he did, the rolling ceased and she felt like herself again. He smiled kindly.

'There's nothing wrong with you, Ray. You're carrying life inside you is all. But you need to take care of yourself, of both of you.'

As the days warmed, spring arrived bit by bit. It emerged in the growing warmth of the sun, the new leaves on the trees in the woods, and the sight and sounds of the birds dancing through the sky. Ray's belly got bigger, and as it swelled Pete had no choice but to acknowledge the consequences of his actions. He'd said nothing, unwilling to speak out loud what was happening, as if his silence might somehow stop the inevitable. But he couldn't keep ignoring it. He nodded towards her swollen belly.

'Ray, why didn't you say something?'

'Say what?'

Pete pointed at her belly.

'About that.'

He couldn't bring himself to say the words.

'Oh, I'm not worried about it no more, Pete. I thought I was ill, maybe dying, like I'd eaten something bad. But Earl says it's ok, it's the opposite of that. I'm carrying a life in me.'

Pete looked at Ray with concern.

'But Ray, do you know what that means?'

'It's life, Pete. That's what Earl said. Now I don't know exactly what that means 'cos Earl talks in riddles sometimes. But I know not to worry, ain't that right, Earl?' Ray looked over Pete's shoulder. 'Earl says, you'll do right by me and I ain't got nothing to worry about.'

Pete's face creased with concern. He didn't know what to say and he watched in silence, as Ray turned and walked to the barn. Christ! The girl was pregnant and, from what he'd just heard, she didn't even understand what that meant. And who was Earl? This invisible person she talked to all the time? Hell! He'd have to tell Ma, and Dwain. That news was going to go down like ten pounds of lead. Ma would have to help Ray, for sure. Maybe make her understand what was happening and then help her with the birthing.

Ma never said nothing when he came out to see Ray. He still didn't understand her feelings about the girl. It didn't make no sense to him. It was pretty clear what Dwain thought about Ray, though. He hated her. God knows why, but for some reason, he just couldn't stand her. Pete gazed off into the distance, his mind rolling and tumbling, his thoughts chaotic. He stared out at the dry, barren landscape. The arrival of spring should have lifted his spirits; the sounds of the birds, the new growth, bringing hope for the future. Instead, he felt overwhelmed. Tears pricked at the corner of his eyes and for the first time in as long as he could remember, Pete fell to sobbing.

Twenty-eight

Pete caught the bartender's eye and nodded to his glass. That was three he'd had. Better slow down, else he wouldn't be fit to ride back. He sure didn't want to turn up at the ranch drunk.

He remembered his Pa coming home from a night in the saloon. How the tension would build the later it got, with him and Dwain taking turns at the window to watch out for his return. Sometimes, he would be jolly and give the boys an affectionate cuff on the ear, and he would look at his Ma with lust in his eyes and take her into the bedroom. Him and Dwain would grab a biscuit and go outside into the barn and there they'd wait until the fire had burned down, then they would sneak back into the cabin to bed. Other times, mostly, his Pa would be mad. He'd lost money at poker or got into a fight with someone younger and stronger. And then he'd come home and take his anger out on his family. It was always Sally he went for first. But it was Dwain that caught the brunt of it — worse the older he got. It would be Dwain who would push Pete out the cabin door telling him to hide. And Dwain who'd stand in front of Ma to take the beating for her.

'Mind some company?'

Deputy Bo slapped his hand on the bar.

'One for me,' he said, 'and another for Pete here.'

He scattered coins over the counter and turned to face Pete.

'The look on your face says you ain't celebrating.'

Pete retreated from his dark thoughts and turned to Bo.

'Your health Bo,' he said.

He knocked it back, hissing as the fiery liquid etched the back of his throat. He'd known Bo for as long as he could remember. Bo's family had always lived in town, and although he was several years older than Pete, you'd think him much younger. Maybe that's what a softer life got you. Bo had worked in the store, until he'd been hired on as the Sheriff's deputy. Pete wasn't the only man in town who'd laughed at soft-handed Bo becoming the law in town. But Bo'd surprised everyone. He'd never shied away from tough work. And he kept a calm head when upholding the peace in the worst of situations. Pete dropped his glass like an auctioneer's gavel. Hearing the slurring in his voice, he knew that he'd had enough.

'Bo, sometimes life just don't turn out the way you expect it. And we can blame everyone and everything, but we got to be responsible for our own actions. You get me?'

'Guess that's right. But sometimes bad things happen to good people. Like the Crow girl. She may be crazier than a box of snakes, but she didn't deserve what happened to her.'

Bo searched for the right words.

'Reckon sometimes when bad things happen to people, it can make them turn bad and thems what cares for them too. Do things they wouldn't normally do.'

Pete struggled to focus on Bo's words. To be clear what he was implying. But too much whiskey slowed his thinking, made his brain into corn mush. He glared at Bo, impatience building.

'Bo, what you trying to say? Why don't you stop talking round the fence post and just come out and tell me what's on your mind.'

'Well Pete, what I'm saying is, that maybe the Crow girl did kill those fellas all them months ago. That maybe you wasn't entirely right in what you was saying to the Sheriff. Cos the thing is Pete, if she didn't do it, then you're the only other one who had reason. And you were out all night and the only person attesting to your whereabouts was Ray Crow. And everyone knows you're close. So, maybe you just decided to deal out some frontier justice.'

Bo let the accusation hang in the silence.

He waved to the bartender for more whiskey. Before Pete could stop him, his glass was full again. He felt his head swim with the alcohol and Bo's words. He thought back to that night. Ray wasn't at the cabin when he got there, and she'd turned up a while after he'd heard the distant gunshots. How long after, he didn't know, having fallen asleep in front of the fire. He'd asked Ray what she'd been doing, and she'd not answered directly. Her explanation hadn't added up then; it still didn't. He'd been trying to avoid even thinking about it. Drunk he may be, stupid he wasn't, or so he thought. He turned back to Bo.

'I don't know what else I can say to you. Besides, it was months ago and I ain't heard no more about it.'

Bo held his peace. He stared at Pete who seemed to be wrestling with his thoughts. The silence dragged on, until Pete couldn't help but speak.

'It's just like I said back at the ranch. I was over at the Crow place with Ray. Ma and Dwain sent me over there to check on her, and that's just what I did. I heard the gunshots, but me and Ray was there at the cabin when it happened.'

Bo gestured to the bartender again, but this time Pete was quick enough to cover his glass.

'Pete,' said Bo, 'when the Sheriff asked, you said you didn't hear no gunshots. So did Ray. But now you're saying that you did. I don't know, Pete. Did you or didn't you?'

'Maybe I heard the gunshots or maybe I didn't, Bo! I'm full up on whiskey and I can't really remember what I heard. But I'm telling you that me and Ray were in that cabin when those two fellas got shot.'

'Maybe you and Ray was busy then, Pete, and that's why you can't remember?'

Pete turned to look at Bo square on.

'What exactly are you driving at Deputy?'

'Oh, I'm just spit balling is all Pete, no need to get on your high horse. You and Ray Crow seem pretty close, and I'm just thinking what most people might be thinking, that there's a little more going on than should be.'

Pete glared at Bo. He was drunk; his anger was rising, and he felt a strong desire to knock Bo on his ass. But he had just enough of his wits left to know that would be a very bad idea. Pounding on a sheriff's deputy would mean a night in the jail and he didn't want that. Pete stood and grabbed his hat from the bar. Squaring his shoulders, he tried to walk away in a straight line. As he reached the doors of the saloon, he resisted the urge to turn and offer some final words to Bo. Instead, he simply exited into the cool night air. After some fumbling with the reins, he managed to unhitch his mare. Dragging himself into the saddle, he started off on the ride home, Bo's last words acting as slow poison in his head.

He rode a slow and meandering path to the ranch. He could feel the chill night air battling with the alcohol. But he knew he wouldn't be sober by the time he got home. His mind whirled, thoughts ricocheting off each other in a kaleidoscope of possibilities. Fragments that remained frustratingly out of reach, always with Ray at the centre. His head whirled and his stomach rolled. He clutched at his belly, groaning, before leaning to the side and vomiting the contents of his guts onto the ground. Pete raised his head feeling the cool breeze pass across his face. He wiped the sour dregs of vomit from his chin and tried to focus.

By the time he reached the ranch, he'd vomited twice more, and his stomach had settled, but his mind was still in turmoil. He didn't relish a confrontation with Ma or Dwain, so after he'd settled the mare in the barn, he laid down in the straw, took off his holster, put his hat over his face and drifted into a drunken sleep.

Pete had no idea how long he slept. He woke up to a sharp pain in his leg. He tried to roll to his side when another blow arrived, and then another. Pete scrabbled about, trying to rise, but his mind and body were dulled by the whiskey. He resorted to curling up into a ball covering his head with his arms waiting for the blows to stop. Eventually, they ceased, and he could hear Dwain drop onto the floor next to him breathing hard. Pete rolled up to sit and stared at Dwain; he looked just like their Pa did. His mouth a hard thin line and his eyes set angry, like he was carrying a world of hurt inside and he was just worn out fighting it.

'Where the fuck you been?' hissed Dwain.

'Town,' mumbled Pete.

He moved gingerly, feeling his ribs. Dwain had sure laid into him, but nothing felt broken, and he hadn't done any real damage. He grimaced to himself. Clearly Dwain's heart wasn't in it; the state he was in, Dwain could have killed him easy, if he'd wanted.

'I was at Ray's, then I was in town. Stopped by the saloon.'

'You didn't spend the night at the Crow place then?' asked Dwain.

'No, I just told you. I was in town, then I got back and slept here where you just found me and gave me a pounding.'

Dwain stood and stared down at his brother, who looked every inch like a man who'd drunk way too much whiskey.

'You need to say away from the Crow place brother. You done enough for that bitch. This whole family's done plenty enough and we don't need the likes of her around.'

Pete avoided Dwain's eyes, focusing on his boots instead. He thought of Ray, her rounded belly with his child inside. He thought of Bo's words. He thought about the night of the gunshots.

What the hell had she done?

He dropped his head into his hands, tears pricking his eyes. Dwain's boot nudged his leg.

'Get up. Go get yourself cleaned up. Ma don't need this.'

Pete raised his head, watching Dwain leave the barn. Then he wiped his face clean and pulled himself up on his feet. His stomach rolled, but there was nothing left to bring up. He walked unsteadily across the dirt to the cabin, pushing thoughts of Ray and dead cowboys from his head.

'You look a mess, son. Take a seat and I'll fix you some breakfast.' Sally looked at Pete and wrinkled her nose. 'Second thoughts, perhaps you better take yourself for a wash before eating.'

'No food, Ma. Just coffee.' Pete lowered himself into a chair and tried to smile. 'Stomach's not so good this morning, too much whiskey.' He gave a small, wry laugh. 'Serves me right, huh Ma?'

Sally sat opposite.

'Something troubling you, son? It's not like you to spend your time drinking in the saloon.'

Pete sipped his coffee in silence. He needed to tell Ma about Ray, about the baby. She was a woman; she'd understand about things like that and they were going to need her help. It was either Ma or the Doc, and if he told the Doc, it'd be all over town in a minute. He could just leave it, say nothing, but then what would happen to Ray? He looked up to see Ma looking directly at him, concern etching fresh lines on her face.

'Ma, thing is. It's Ray.'

Pete watched her expression alter. The concern was still there, but there was something else he couldn't identify. She shifted back in her chair slightly.

'Go on.'

Pete took a breath.

'Ma, Ray's with child.'

Sally gasped, colour drained from her face. Her hands flew to her mouth. She couldn't believe what her son had just said.

Ray's pregnant!

She felt sick.

Her first thought: it was the cowboys that attacked her. But she knew by the look on Pete's face what she most dreaded was true. It was him. She could see the fear and turmoil in his eyes. He looked at her pleading for her help and understanding. Sally leapt to her feet, her chair scraping back and falling to the ground. She spun away from Pete, trying to slow her breathing, to clear her mind. After a while she turned back, her voice sharp and brittle.

'Son, when did this happen? How far gone is she?'

'I'm thinking it's nigh on six months, Ma. But she don't really understand what's happening to her. I'm scared for her and what'll happen when the baby's ready to come. We need your help, Ma.'

'What do you mean, she don't understand? Are you saying she don't know she's pregnant?'

'She keeps telling me she's carrying a life, but I'm not sure she understands that means she's carrying a baby in her.'

'Pete, if she don't understand that, does she understand how that baby got there?'

Pete looked down at the table, his hands gripping the coffee cup tighter. Sally stared at him, waiting for a response. There was nothing but silence. She felt anger building from the pit of her stomach. Unbidden feelings and memories rising. She tried to squash them down, but they were unstoppable. She could see her own rapist's ugly face above her, and she remembered her pain and fear. But her son couldn't have done that to a woman, could he? Not Pete. He was so kind and gentle.

Sally's voice went cold. It held all her pain, and her words came mean from her mouth.

'Son, did you take that girl against her will?'

Pete raised his head and spoke softly.

'No Ma. It wasn't like that.'

But his face made a liar of him. His eyes held his shame. Sally flew across the table at him, raining blows. Pete covered his head with his hands. She heard herself screaming, as she whaled on her son, as hard as she could. Cries of pain and anger burst out of her until abruptly she was spent. Her anger retreated fast as it had come, leaving a leaden sadness. She collapsed into a chair, hot, heavy tears rolling down her face. Leaning across the table she took hold of Pete's hands. He raised his head, seeing her tears reflecting her thoughts.

She saw everything inside him. His pain, shame and fear. She couldn't tell him about Ray, who she was. She'd have to deal with that herself. She would need to be strong for her son.

Twenty-nine

The Sheriff leaned back in his chair, feet on the desk, listening to Bo repeating his conversation with Pete Mickleton from the night before. It was clear Pete had been drunk, and Bo had helped that along, but that didn't necessarily make Pete's words any less true. Although, whiskey and reliability didn't generally go hand in hand.

He remembered clearly Pete and Ray denying they'd heard any gunshots on the night Cole and Audley had died. The Sheriff hadn't believed them at the time. It was obvious, they'd have heard something if they were at the Crow place. Sound carries a long way in those parts and the bodies were found not more than an hour's ride from the homestead. Their denial just tickled at his senses. Hell, if they'd just said they heard the gunshots and were curious or scared, he'd have believed them and likely his suspicions wouldn't have been raised. But then again, they probably would. He always said, every good sheriff needs a suspicious mind.

He turned his attention back to his deputies, Bo on his toes and keen as always, Jim leaning back against the wall, playing it cool. The Sheriff stood and started to pace. He thought better on the move. After a time, he spoke.

'Boys, I reckon Bo has a point. Sounds to me like Pete and Ray were lying when they said they didn't hear no gunshots. If they lied about that, means they had a reason to. And the only reason I can think of is that one, or both of them, fired those gunshots. But that still don't solve this mystery, does it?'

He resumed his pacing. Bo and Jim held their silence, assuming correctly the Sheriff was speaking hypothetically.

'Now boys, I figure the question is, which one of them shot those assholes, and which one is covering it up for the other? I don't think the girl has it in her to kill someone in cold blood like that. I wouldn't have said Pete had it in him neither. But sometimes people do things you wouldn't expect, and my gut feeling is that

Pete has some strong feelings for that girl and if someone hurt her, he'd pretty much do anything to look out for her. Even if that meant killing.'

Jim stepped forward to catch the Sheriff's eye.

'Boss, so you're saying you think they both did it. Together like?'

'I'm not saying they did or they didn't, just that they could have. Or else Pete did it on his own. Maybe, he was heading over to the Crow place, when he saw you heading those cowboys out of town?'

'I didn't see him Boss,' said Jim. 'I'd have told you if I did.'

The Sheriff held up a reassuring hand.

'Just thinking out loud here, Jim. But, maybe Pete did see you, or maybe he picked up from one of his boys that you was going to be heading them out of town. But anyhow, just say that he saw, and he followed, and once they were alone and asleep, he crept on in there and put a bullet in them. Then he gets back on his horse and rides over to the Crow place.'

'That makes sense, Sheriff,' said Bo. 'And I reckon that Ray would lie to protect Pete.'

Sheriff Boone perched on the edge of his desk.

'Boys, I don't know about you, but I'd pretty much put this mystery to the back corner, until now. It's true, I ain't mourning the loss of those cowboys, but I'll not ignore murder in my town, even if it did happen a while ago. I'll do what needs to be done, whenever I can.'

The Sheriff stood, grabbing his hat from his desk and ramming it on his head.

'I think maybe Bo, you and I'll head out to the Mickleton's, and have ourselves another talk with Pete, and see what comes of it.'

As Sheriff Boone and Deputy Bo approached the ranch, the sun was high in the sky and the dust thick on the ground. Both men squinted through the glare, as the ranch took shape in front of them. The air was still and Bo thought the place looked empty. He was glad he lived in town; it felt barren and lonely out here. He wasn't surprised that the people who lived out here became as hard as the ground they farmed. He turned to look at the Sheriff, sitting relaxed in the saddle. Sheriff Boone felt Bo's eyes on him and spoke without turning his head.

'C'mon son, let's get this over with. I don't expect Dwain will be here, no doubt he's out seeing to his cattle, but maybe Pete will be, if he was as drunk last night as you said he was.'

Their horses kicked up plumes of dust crossing the yard to the ranch house. They dismounted and the Sheriff yelled a greeting.

'Hey, you in there. Sheriff Boone and Deputy Bo here. Anyone home?'

They hitched their horses to the rail outside and made to step onto the veranda when Sally came out. The Sheriff took in her appearance and he hoped Bo would make the same observation as him. Sally had lost weight and she looked tired. Her face was etched with tension, the lines on her face deeper than he ever remembered. Something was definitely not right out at the Mickleton ranch, that was clear. Sally wiped her hands on her apron.

'Sheriff. Bo. I wasn't expecting you.'

'Well, we weren't planning on making a visit Sally, but Bo spent some time with Pete last night and, well, it got me pondering a few things. On account of that, I thought we'd ride out and have a word or two.'

Sally glanced back into the cabin. The Sheriff reckoned Pete would be sitting inside nursing his hangover. He smiled at Sally, tipping his hat back on his head.

'Bo and I are mighty thirsty, Sally. It was a hot, dry ride out here. Perhaps, I could trouble you to put a pot of coffee on and send Pete out?'

Sally nodded and turned back into the cabin. A few moments later, Pete appeared in the doorway. He'd clearly not bathed, or slept much, and he didn't smell too good neither.

'Pete Mickleton, you sure look like a man who filled up on whiskey last night.'

Pete leant against the wall, hands in his pockets, trying to look nonchalant and failing. He nodded at the Sheriff and turned his gaze on Bo before speaking.

'So, Bo, I'm guessing you're here 'cos you went straight back to your boss after filling me with whiskey last night and trying to trick me into confessing to something I didn't do.'

'Now Pete,' said the Sheriff. 'There's no need for that kind of attitude. Bo here did talk to me, but only 'cos he had some concerns that you hadn't been entirely honest with us the last time we spoke. So, I'm here to ask you again: where were you when Cole and Audley got shot?'

Pete responded without hesitation, keeping his gaze on Bo.

'Like I told you both, I was at Ray Crow's place all night. I don't know what time I left here, but it was still light. By the time I got to the Crow place, it was dark. That's it.'

'And son, while you were at the Crow place, did you hear gunshots?'

Before Pete could respond Sally appeared with two mugs of coffee. The Sheriff stepped forward taking both mugs and passing one to Bo. After Sally handed over the coffee, she hovered in the doorway. She looked anxious, her gaze constantly shifting between Pete and Sheriff Boone. The Sheriff waited patiently for Pete's response.

'Thank you, Sally, this is a fine coffee, ain't that right, Bo?'

'Yes, it is, thank you, Ma'am.'

'Well, Pete can you answer my question?'

Pete appeared to slouch a little more against the wall, his shoulders slumping. His voice was flat when he answered.

'Yes, Sheriff, I did hear gun shots, two of them in fact. The first caught me by surprise, then I heard a second one, straight after.'

'Why didn't you say that when I first asked you. Although, if I remember correctly, it was Ray that answered for you both.'

Pete looked downcast, glancing first at his Ma and then down at his feet before responding.

'I don't know, Sheriff, I guess it all took me by surprise. The questioning that is.' Pete looked directly at the Sheriff. 'But I didn't kill those men Sheriff. I was surprised to hear they was dead.'

'What about Ray then, Pete. Was she with you when you heard the gunshots?'

Pete continued to look at the Sheriff, but this time there was a pause before he answered.

'Yes sir, she was.'

Thirty

Sally watched from the veranda as the wagon arrived with Pete and Ray side by side on the bench. Her body was tight with tension and her head ached from the weight of it. Dwain had made sure he wasn't at home for their arrival, and she couldn't blame him.

The strength of his reaction when he'd been told about the baby had been frightening. His face contorted with rage; she'd felt the full force of his anger coming off him in waves. He was unable to speak; emotion jamming the words in his throat. He'd walked out, not returning until the following day. Since then, her boys barely spoke. They'd continued their work on the ranch, with Pete regularly riding out to Ray's place to check on her, always under the disapproving glare of his brother. Sally had soaked up all that tension until her skin crawled and her stomach was tied in knots.

As the cart came to a halt, Pete jumped to the ground and ran around the other side to help Ray down. Sally took in Ray's appearance as she stepped down to the ground. Her hair was growing back fast and had matted again. It reached down past her chin and fanned out in clumps from underneath the hat jammed on her head. She was clearly with child, although she was still wearing pants cinched underneath the mound of her belly. She walked with a slow, calm stride toward the cabin. As she got closer Sally could see the expression on her face; it was almost beatific. As she walked, she turned and motioned behind her, as if there was someone else there, and then she began to laugh, as if sharing a joke.

Sally looked toward Pete with concern. Something didn't feel right and the look on her son's face confirmed it. Pete tenderly placed his hand on Ray's back as she climbed up the steps onto the veranda. As she approached, it was clear to Sally she had cause for concern. Although Ray looked serene at first glance, even happy, up close the expression on her face was that of a child. It spoke of ignorance, rather than acceptance and joy. Sally held her hand out to Ray.

'Come on girl, let's get you inside.'

She took Ray's hand, led her through the door and once inside, guided her into a chair. The expression on Ray's face didn't change. Her lips were fixed into half a smile, but her eyes were unfocused, as if her mind was far away.

'Have you eaten?' Sally asked. Ray didn't respond, but Pete shook his head.

'No Ma, I ain't and I don't think Ray has either.'

'I got some stew here on the stove, I'll fix you some.'

Sally ladled out two steaming bowls. As she placed them on the table she watched Ray carefully. The blankness in her eyes remained. But every now and then she would smile or gesture, as if she was listening to something or someone. Sally looked at Pete, questioning, but he just shook his head before tucking into his stew.

Once they'd eaten, Sally guided Ray into her bedroom and gestured to the cot she'd placed there for her.

'Why don't you settle yourself down for the night girl. You need your sleep now, while you can get it.'

Ray turned to Sally, addressing her directly for the first time.

'Thanks Sally. It's all going to be OK you know. Earl says we need new life, and Pete will look after me. It's Dwain I got to watch. He killed my horse you know. He'll probably try to kill me, but Pete won't let him. Ain't that right?'

'Who's Earl?' said Sally.

'He's my friend; he looks out for me. He says you're my family now and you'll look out for me too.'

Sally's face hardened.

'What do you mean we're your family? What's this Earl been saying to you?'

Ray turned, smiling at Sally.

'He says we're family, so we're going to stick together. And my little sister, when she comes.'

Ray looked down and stroked her belly before looking up at Sally again, eyes shining.

Sally tore her gaze from Ray. And with legs shaking she left the room. She eased her fragile body into a chair. Her vision began to tunnel, and she couldn't get her breath. Blackness gathered around her. And then Dwain was there calling her.

'Ma, Ma! What's wrong Ma!'

He sounded panicked and began shaking her. The darkness receded. She opened her mouth, sucking in air. Her vision cleared, but the shaking remained. Dwain thrust a cup of water into her trembling hands.

'Here Ma, drink this. Go on, drink.'

He watched with concern, as Sally sipped from the cup. She felt her body begin to calm. Looking up at Dwain, she gave him a weak smile.

'It's OK. I think I just had a funny turn is all. I'm fine now.'

Dwain sat opposite, taking her hands in his.

'Shit, Ma! You had me worried then. I thought you was dying.'

'No son,' she said, 'just tired. Not been sleeping well lately.'

Dwain looked toward the bedroom, face hardening.

'Having that girl here ain't going to fix that is it Ma? I don't know why you encouraged Pete to bring her here. She should have stayed at her own place. She ain't our problem.'

He released Sally's hands, forming fists of anger and frustration.

Sally shook her head. What could she say? Of course Ray was her problem. And the child that she would bear from incest was her problem too. Yes, it was her problem to deal with, but how? She'd not left the ranch in twenty years. Even stepping off the veranda was a challenge. Her heart would race, her head start to spin, and her legs would feel so weak they would give way; that wasn't going to change now.

Over the next few days, Sally thought long and hard about what she needed to do and how she might accomplish it. Eventually, she realised she would need help, and it was Pete she turned to.

'Pete, I need you to fetch the Doc out here to see Ray.'

Pete frowned, shaking his head.

'No Ma, we can't do that. She's crazier than ever at the moment and I don't know how the Doc's going to react to that. Besides, he'll just go and tell Sheriff Boone about the pregnancy and that won't look good on me. Can't you just look after her? That's why she's here, ain't it?'

Sally felt some small relief. Pete had responded exactly as she thought he would.

'Well son, thing is, birthing is no easy matter. There's drugs that can help. And around here only the Doc's got them.'

She paused and took a breath before continuing.

'There's some herbs that can help, but you can't just buy them in the general store. Lena Crow used to grow them out at her place, but now she's gone, only other option is to get some from another midwife. There's a woman over in Colton Town, by the name of Ella-Mae. She can help, but you're going to have to go see her for me Pete. You know I can't go.'

Pete's face was a picture of confusion.

'Ma, are you serious? That's two days ride.'

'I know, son, but you got to do it for Ray. You just go into town there and ask for Ella-Mae Reisberg. She's a black woman, learnt the art of birthing when she was a slave. She's free now and lives out of town, but all the women thereabouts know about Ella-Mae. She knew Ray's Ma, Lena too. Her and Lena were on the same train out of Oregon, and she taught Lena everything she knew. I know it Pete, 'cos Lena told me once. She'll help, I know she will.'

Pete stood to face his Ma.

'And what about payment, what's these herbs going to cost?'

'Just tell her it's for Lena's girl, Pete. And tell her you're the father. She'll help. I'm sure of it.

Thirty-one

Pete arrived in Colton; exhaustion weighing heavy on him. He'd ridden hard. He and his mount were brown with dust like they were formed out of the same earth. As he travelled down Main Street disappointment crept up on him. The town looked dull and thoroughly uncared for. Dust devils spiralled down the dirt street chasing tumbleweeds. Wind made eerie whistling sounds as it passed between ramshackle buildings.

Pete dismounted at the General Store, looping his reins over a hitching post. Inside, the only customer was a lady in a well-patched blue dress. As he entered, she moved aside wrinkling her nose and clutching her skirts. Approaching the counter, Pete cleared a voice parched with dust and asked the storekeeper after the whereabouts of Ella-Mae Reisberg. The man glared at Pete and spat on the packed dirt floor.

'That Ella-Mae is one notorious witch,' he said, 'and where she abides is no business of a Christian.'

Pete considered drawing his pistol and aiming the barrel at the man's head. Perhaps that'd make him a bit more cooperative. But if he caused a ruckus, whatever passes for the law in this two-bit town would be making an appearance. No, he'd best look to someone else for directions.

Pete stood outside the store pondering his next move. Then he noticed the woman from the store had crossed to the opposite side of the street. She was looking left and right and beckoning him to her. Pete crossed the street.

'You're looking for Ella-Mae?' asked the woman.

'Sure am,' rasped Pete.

'You need to head out of town that way,' she said, pointing to the far end of town. 'And after about a fifteen-minute ride, you'll see a track to the right. Take it and head on 'long that way for a while until you reach a stand of trees. Then you want to take the left track through them, and you'll see Ella's place up ahead. She don't take much to strangers, but she ain't no witch.'

With that, the woman ducked past Pete, hurrying away without a backward glance. He muttered thanks to her back and returned to his horse. Leaving Main Street he followed the woman's directions.

He reached Ella-Mae's place. It took the form of a wooden shack in a grove of buttonwood trees. The branches of which were decorated with lengths of ribbon and rope. They floated in the breeze, a rainbow of colours contrasting with the drabness of the surroundings.

Pete rode up to the shack. The door was daubed with intricate curlicue symbols. There were wood carvings positioned along the path. Strange, rounded shapes which made no sense to him. Perhaps the woman really was a witch. Exhaustion and thirst removed any fears. Witch or no witch, he hoped she'd at least offer him some water. He stood high in the stirrups checking the lie of the land. It was cooler in the shadow of the trees. He was shocked to find the sun so low in the sky. It would be dark soon and he'd have to be picking out a place to make camp. His attention returned to the shack. The door was open now and a tall heavyset black woman was scrutinising him.

'You Ella-Mae Reisberg?'

'Who wants to know?' she said, wiping her hands on a grease-stained apron.

'Come from Sally Mickleton,' said Pete.

'You look fit to drop from the saddle, boy. Tie up your horse and come on in.'

Pete did as she told him and followed her inside. For such a big woman Ella-Mae moved with a stately grace. He didn't know what to expect. It certainly wasn't this homely, tranquil room. She grunted, pointing to a chair and fetched him a tin mug of water.

'Drink slowly boy, or you get belly ache. Then you go water that poor ol' horse a yours. When you've done that,' she chuckled, 'I'll offer you something a might stronger'n water.'

When Pete returned he checked out the room. The shack was bigger than it looked from the outside. On one side herbs hung in big bunches from the ceiling and a table held wooden bowls filled with dried flowers and seed pods. The smell was sweet and cloying, but not unpleasant. He sat at the table. Ella-Mae placed a steaming mug of coffee and a mason jar of clear liquid in front of him, then took a seat opposite.

'You're not familiar to me, son. And I don't know no Sally Mickleton. But you look like you've had a hard ride, so I expect you're not from around here. That means you've ridden a ways to see me. Care to tell me what it is you want?' Pete blew steam from the top of his mug before taking a sip. He'd have the corn liquor in a while.

'Storekeeper told me you're a witch.'

Ella-Mae chortled.

'Hell, they think that 'cos that's what I make them think. You live in a cabin out of town, put a few ribbons in the trees and some swirly paint on the door, and there you go, people think you're a witch.'

Pete looked into Ella-Mae's twinkling eyes. The woman was shrewd, he could see that, but so was he.

'Oh, I don't think that's enough to make townsfolk think you're a witch, Ma'am.'

The smile dropped from Ella-Mae's face.

'No son, it's not. I expect that's why you rode all this way.'

Pete nodded and, after taking another sip of coffee, he told Ella-Mae as best he could about Ray, and what his Ma had said. Ella-Mae closed her eyes for a few seconds, as if saying a silent prayer, before she spoke again.

'I'm sorry to hear Lena's passed. I knew her well and considered her a good friend. We was on the same train together out of Oregon over twenty years ago, and I taught her everything I knew about herbs, and women's health, birthing and all that. We had some work to do on that journey, caring for folks.'

She shook her head as if to disperse bad memories.

'And you're talking about Lena Crow's girl, Ray? And you're Sally Mickleton's boy, the younger one?'

Pete nodded.

'Mmmhh, I know Ray and I know of you son, and your family, now's I think about it. Although I've never met your Ma. Lena always came out to see me couple of times a year, and she'd bring her girl when she was little. That girl was special you know son. A child of the spirits. She used to play with my boy Earl. Although he was older than her, running through the trees, her hair flying behind her and a smile so wide you'd have thought it would take the top of her head off.'

Ella-Mae paused, holding the memory for as long as she could. She reached across, taking the jar of liquor and putting it down in front of Pete, looking at him intently.

'She's pregnant and you're the father?'

'Yes Ma'am,' he said quietly, lowering his head.

'Mmmhhh. I see son, I see.'

Ella-Mae reached across the table to lay a rough hand on Pete's. She looked hard at him with a sadness in her eyes that made Pete's heart heavy.

'Drink the liquor. I'll be busy for some time getting things ready for you. When you've finished I suggest you go and lay down on the cot over there and get some sleep. I'll wake you when I'm ready.'

When Pete awoke dawn was breaking and Ella-Mae was preparing breakfast, humming a tune. He had no idea whether Ella-Mae had slept, but she seemed as fresh as if she'd had a night of sweet dreams. She smiled at him as he got up and gestured for him to take a seat at the table. A few minutes later, she placed a plate of beans and bacon in front of him. After he'd eaten, Ella-Mae handed him a small cloth bag.

'Son, keep this dry no matter what. It needs to stay good and dry, d'you understand me?'

'Yes Ma'am.'

Pete took the bag, feeling the weight of the herbs in his hand.

'Tell your Ma when the time is right, steep this in boiling water to make a tea. Ray needs to drink every drop of it, do you hear me?'

'Yes Ma'am, I hear you.'

'Good, son. She's a special girl, that Ray. She's not meant for a life like yours. You know that now, don't you?'

Pete nodded.

'I think I do, Ma'am.'

As he rode off, he glanced back and saw Ella-Mae still standing in the doorway watching him, her ribbons floating in the breeze, bright and colourful. A wave of sadness came over him.

He turned back to the track, hunched down in the saddle, and began the long ride home.

Thirty-two

Seeing the shimmering shape of the ranch in the distance, Pete breathed a sigh of relief. He was thirsty. His mouth felt like a dust bowl. There was grit in his eyes and up his nose. Over every part of him. His horse walked like she was wading through quicksand. He patted her neck, speaking gentle words of encouragement.

'There it is girl, there's home. Just a bit further and its water and a long rest for you.'

He'd ridden hard to get home. He could feel the weight of the herbs he carried: the burden of responsibility and the fear of what would happen over the coming days. He felt drawn to Ray like nothing else, a compulsion to have her and hold her, even if her mind seemed to be unravelling as the days went on. He felt the need to hold on to her tight, because if he didn't, she might just break apart into dust and blow away on the wind. He'd do whatever was needed to protect her and his baby.

When he arrived Ma was somewhere in the cabin and Dwain was sitting on the veranda. He'd made good time and was lucky to get home before dark. He wanted nothing more than to drink, wash, and eat, in that order. But he'd see to his horse first. He rode past the house and straight to the barn. Pumping up a bucket of water for the horse, he scooped some into his mouth, before putting it down for her.

Dwain appeared in the doorway. Pete couldn't remember the last time he'd seen Dwain smile. Ever since his Pa died, Dwain had been sullen and angry. The only time he showed any tenderness was when he was with Ma. Dwain had always cared for her; had always been there to protect her. He wondered why Dwain couldn't understand that's what he wanted to do for Ray. Care for her and protect her.

'Where you been?'

Pete sighed. He was tired and felt as if he was carrying the weight of the world on his shoulders. The last thing he needed was Dwain getting on his case.

'Dwain, I ain't in the mood for a fight. I got to rub down the horse. Then I'd just like to get myself washed and fed before I get me a good night's sleep. It's been a long couple of days.'

'That ain't answering my question.'

Dwain moved into the barn and stood, legs wide, his stance combative.

'You just up and leave the ranch to me, no word. Ma's not telling me nothing. I want to know where you been. This got something to do with the crazy pregnant bitch?'

Pete felt anger rising. Dwain'd no right to talk about Ray like that. She'd never done anything to hurt him. He hauled off the mare's saddle. Grabbing a curry comb he began running it over the mare's back.

'The Doc's been out here while you been gone, you hear. One of the ranch hands must have said something in the saloon about her being here and it got back to the Doc. Said he was worried she weren't well, having to come out and live at our place again. So, now he knows she's pregnant, but that ain't all he knows. Ma heard them talking Pete. She heard Ray saying all sorts of stuff to the Doc.'

Pete stopped grooming his horse, tossing the comb away, before moving to confront Dwain.

'What sort of stuff you talking about Dwain? What's got you so riled up?'

Dwain wrestled with his thoughts before speaking, his tone slipping from anger to concern.

'She was talking to the Doc about Cole and Audley. About what they did to her. About how it wasn't right, and how they deserved to pay for what they done. She told the Doc she heard the gunshots out at her cabin, before you arrived. Said you wasn't with her, that you were with me, doing fuck knows what. And you can bet anything if'n Ray told the Doc, he gone done told the Sheriff. Now I know I didn't do nothing to those cowboys, but you... Pete you need to tell me what's going on. Really going on. I can't protect you, if I don't know nothin.'

Pete's worse fears came bubbling to the surface. He

remembered walking across the yard at Ray's homestead and hearing the gunshots echoing from the hills, their sound sharp in the quiet of the night. The cabin standing empty in the darkness. He remembered Ray turning up later, her eyes bright and feverish with no decent explanation of where she'd been.

'I didn't do it, Dwain. I mean, I wanted to kill them for what they did to her, but I didn't, I wouldn't. But I did hear it happen, I think. I got to the homestead and Ray wasn't there. I put my horse in the barn and was heading to the cabin when I heard those shots, first one, then the other. Ray turned up a while later.'

Dwain moved closer to Pete. His face was etched deep with the harshness of life, making him look far older than his years.

'Do you think she did it, Pete?'

His voice was flat and devoid of emotion. It contained no challenge. No spite to needle his brother into rising up in Ray's defence.

Pete's response mirrored his brother's question, flat and empty.

'Don't know Dwain. But I think she may well have.'

'You need to go into town tomorrow and tell the Sheriff Pete. This situation is fucked up man.'

Pete caught the emotion flooding back into Dwain's voice.

'You don't know all of it Pete. But that girl shouldn't be here. She's nothing but poison to this family. Always has been. You shouldn't be with her; it's just plain wrong.'

'What, 'cos she's crazy, mad, as you keep saying Dwain?' His voice was rising. 'She's done nothing to you, Dwain. Nothing! I don't know why you hate her so much; it's not like it's her fault her Pa killed ours.'

Dwain spat out words full of pain and wrath.

'She killed our Pa years ago! She shouldn't never have lived.'

Turning on his heel, he strode out into the cool evening air.

Pete ran after him — thirst and hunger forgotten.

'What are you saying Dwain, what the fuck are you saying?'

Pete grabbed Dwain's shoulder spinning him round.

'Dwain, what the fuck are you saying?'

Dwain's face crumpled, the anger melting, leaving lines etched with sadness and eyes shining with tears. Pete saw Dwain's tough shell crumble. All that was left was the boy he'd played with. The kid that took beatings to protect him, when Pa's anger overflowed. Inside, he realised Dwain was still the same as he had always been. Scared and brave all at the same time. Pete's anger dissipated. He grabbed Dwain's shoulders and looked him in the eye.

'Dwain, what is it, tell me.'

'I can't Pete, I can't.' Dwain's voice was flat. 'Go see the Sheriff tomorrow, Pete. Just tell him the truth. Things are in motion now Pete and you can't stop them. It's too late.'

Dwain turned and walked back to the cabin. Pete stood and watched him go, his steps laboured, carrying his hurt, his fear and his anger on his broad shoulders. He knew Dwain was right and he should go and see the Sheriff, but he also knew he wouldn't. He couldn't do that to Ray.

Taking a deep breath he squared his shoulders and followed Dwain inside.

Thirty-three

As spring transitioned into summer, life at the Mickleton ranch continued its relentless pace. Dwain and Pete worked their cattle on the spread and on Ray's abutting homestead. Dwain had annexed most of Ray's land and the cattle were benefiting from the extra grazing. Pete, though, was sure the herd wouldn't last for much longer if they didn't see some rain. What grass there was, speared through the dirt, yellow and stunted. Dwain had butchered one of the undernourished cows and the meat was too tight and lean to make good eating. Ray's land was more sand than soil. The burnt cornfield remained barren and dry, and Lena's old herb garden, which had once been a green oasis, was brown and bare.

There was an uneasy truce at the ranch. Sally looked after Ray, who spent her days in the barn and her nights alone in the bedroom. Dwain and Pete worked in the day and they all ate together at sundown. After eating in silence Dwain and Pete would sit on the veranda with coffee and maybe a whiskey until they retired to the bunkhouse. Pete felt like their lives were on hold. Waiting on the birth of the baby. Waiting for the rain to save them. Waiting for the Sheriff to arrive accusing one of them of murder. Pete didn't think he could stand much more of this waiting. As it turned out he didn't have to.

One hot dry afternoon, much like any other, the brothers returned to the ranch from driving cattle from one parched pasture to another. There was a different sort of tension at the Mickleton's. The atmosphere crackled as it might before a storm. The hairs on Pete's arms stood up. He'd find himself looking over his shoulder, convinced someone was behind him. As was now usual they ate supper in silence. This particular night Pete felt the weight of unspoken words resting heavy between him and Dwain. They swelled his gut with fear till there was no room for food. He ate sparsely and headed to the veranda. Once outside he gulped air like a fish on a riverbank. Dwain didn't join him on the veranda after the meal. He made his way to the bunkhouse without a look or a word. Did he think Pete needed to be alone? More likely he simply didn't want his brother's company. It was all the same to Pete. Standing there watching the sun disappear he felt the tension begin to dissipate. He hoped that tomorrow would bring respite. But in his heart of hearts he knew it wouldn't.

Ray woke early, the sun had yet to appear on the horizon. She hadn't slept well. Most of the night had been spent tossing and turning, slipping in and out of fevered dreams. The cabin was quiet and chill. Sally was asleep, snoring gently in her cot. Ray pulled on her boots and quietly left the room. She went to the barn and breathed in the sweet, familiar musk of horses. In an attempt to shake off the nightmares she began to groom Rain. The repetitive action of the curry comb calmed and reassured her. She brushed Rain until his coat shone and her arms ached. Soon the barn was flooded with morning sunlight and the dreams seemed less substantial. Then...

Something was wrong.

A hot wetness ran down her legs, pooling on the ground. There was a fierce pain. Her belly contracted, doubling her up. Gripping the edge of the stall she slid down until her knees were on the wet ground. She went to scream but her lungs were devoid of air.

'Earl, help me,' she pleaded, her voice strained and weak.

And Earl was there, lifting her up, propelling her to the door of the barn. She saw his wings begin to unfurl as he tried to lift her, but she pulled back. She didn't want to fly, she needed to stay on the ground, in the dirt. On her hands and knees, she dug her fingers into the dust, clawing at the earth. Her stomach contracted and guttural sounds forced their way out of her mouth. She felt the inexorable pull of the sun, as it rose slowly in the sky, attempting to lift her. But she dug further into the hard soil, fingernails splitting, blood staining the brown earth.

Sally began preparing breakfast. She relished time alone without her boys or Ray. The air was clearer and calmer. She could push aside the persistent fear that gnawed at her bones and ate her flesh. She hummed a tune; the light melody brought a shy smile to her face. Then she felt someone behind her, but she'd not heard the door opening. She twisted around, but there was no-one there. As she turned back to the stove a hand descended on her shoulder, and a voice whispered Ray's name. Fear overwhelmed her. She turned slowly, but again the room was empty. The door was now ajar. She dried her hands and went to close it. Glancing outside she saw Ray writhing in the dirt.

Sally raced down the steps, fear of the outdoors forgotten. Ray was in labour. Her breeches were wet and her stomach was contracting. Her expression contorted as wave after wave of agony swept through her. Sally gripped Ray under the arms and attempted lifting her. But she couldn't manage her dead weight, nor loosen the hands clawing at the earth.

'Ray, Ray! We need to get you inside,' Sally screamed. 'Please Ray, please help me!'

Sally heaved at Ray once more. This time, she felt Ray cooperating, her body becoming lighter. She saw something else. Through the confusion of sunlight and shadow there was the faintest shape of another person. Ray tottered to her feet. Supported by Sally on one side and the apparition on the other, Ray struggled into the ranch house and collapsed onto her bed. She groaned, clutching her belly. An effusion of blood soaked into the bedding. Sally felt Ray's forehead; the poor thing was burning up.

'Hold on girl, hold on,' Sally whispered.

She raced to the kitchen and grabbed Ella-Mae's bag of herbs from the cupboard. Stoking the stove, she put a pan of water on to boil. In the bedroom she tugged off Ray's breeches and covered her with a blanket. Then, back at the stove she steeped the herbs in boiling water.

Was it too late?

The baby was nearly there and she'd not fed Ray the tea. This was all happening too fast.

When Sally returned to the bedroom her breathing was still harsh, her eyes glassy and unfocussed. But she was calmer, and no longer writhing and contorting. Sally sat on the edge of the bed. She lifted Ray's head, placing a rolled blanket behind her.

'Ray, sweetheart,' said Sally, 'you have to listen to me. I've made you a drink, it's a special tea, it'll help with the birthing. But I'm going to need you to swallow it all. You hear me girl, you have to drink it all.'

Ray nodded as another contraction wracked her body. Sally

watched the pain travelling through her. Ray's hands clutching at the blanket, tears spilling down her cheeks. After the contraction passed, Ray turned her head as if looking at someone on the other side of the bed. She smiled briefly before her lips became tight and stretched again. Sally placed a hand behind Ray. Lifting her head she guided the mug of tea to her lips.

'Ray you need to drink this. That's it girl, drink it down.'

Sally forced the tea through Ray's lips. She managed to swallow some, but the rest dribbled down her chin. Sally took the cup away and dabbed Ray's mouth with a cloth. She presented it to Ray's lips, again and again, until half the tea was gone. Sally's arm ached from the effort of propping her up. Ray slipped back against the blanket pillow. Sally wrung out a cloth in cool water, and wiped the sweat from Ray's face. Ray tolerated Sally's fussing, her attention still on the other side of the cot.

Sally addressed the shimmering empty space.

'She needs to drink this tea, do you understand? She needs to drink it. It's important.'

Ray turned her head toward Sally. She smiled and Sally smiled back. Once more she supported Ray's head and brought the cup to her lips, slowly letting the liquid trickle down Ray's throat. It wasn't long before the cup was empty.

The labour continued as the sun rose high in the sky, its heat permeating the cabin. Ray bore the pain mostly in silence, save for deep rasping sounds forcing their way out of her throat with each contraction. Sally checked her regularly, but she wasn't yet fully dilated. Sally knew Ray wasn't ready for the baby to come. And if things progressed for much longer, Ray's life would hang in the balance. By the afternoon, Ray was exhausted, drifting in and out of consciousness, rising to the surface during each contraction and then dropping under again.

Sally stroked her forehead and spoke gentle words of encouragement. The contractions were getting closer. Another hour passed, then two, she checked Ray again. The baby was nearly ready to come. Sally felt relief for Ray. She fetched more water and clean cloths, wiping the damp rags across Ray's face to refresh and rouse her. She called her name again and again, louder each time. A huge contraction tore through Ray's body and her eyes flew open.

'Push', shouted Sally. 'Push, you got to push this baby out!'

She gripped Ray's hand, squeezing hard, feeling Ray's strength squeezing back. Ray opened her mouth and let out a high-pitched scream, like the call of a bird. Ray's body rose up, as if weightless, borne aloft by something Sally couldn't see.

Darkness flooded the room, and as Sally looked up, she could see the outline of giant feathers spread across the ceiling. Ray's body twisted and turned, contorting in the air, as she continued to scream; her back arched till Sally thought it would break. Abruptly the tension left her and Ray was once again recumbent on the bed. The blood-soaked body of a tiny baby slid softly into the blankets.

Seconds later, the darkness lifted and the late afternoon light flooded into the room once more. The air felt clear and calm. Ray lay still, breathing softly, eyes closed. Sally gently lifted the baby, clearing the fluid from its face. It was slick with blood, its eyes closed, but it was whole and breathing, a soft whistling coming from its tiny mouth. Sally's thoughts rolled and tumbled into one another. She couldn't think. She didn't want to think.

She wrapped the baby in a clean blanket and walked out of the cabin, down onto the yard and across to the barn. It was cool and quiet in there, the soft late afternoon light dulled the edges of things, casting a soft pink glow. She gently placed the baby on a pile of straw. Then she kissed its forehead tenderly, and walked back to the cabin.

Thirty-four

Pete and Dwain arrived back at the ranch as the sun was sitting low in the sky, casting its soft light over the land. Pete looked across to his brother, concern etched on his face. Something didn't feel right. The ranch felt empty. The door to the cabin was ajar and swinging in the evening breeze. There was no smoke from the chimney to welcome them home. Unspoken words passed between them.

They urged their horses faster. Reaching the cabin they dismounted and threw their reins over the rail. They stepped onto the veranda, hands on their guns, ready for anything. Dwain entered the cabin first. He scanned the darkening interior. Ma was slumped at the table, head resting on her hands as if asleep. Fear clutched at him as he tentatively touched her shoulder.

'Ma, you OK?' he whispered.

Sally raised her head sleepily, giving him a weak smile. Dwain and Pete looked at each other. The air was metallic with the taint of blood and sweat. Dwain nodded toward the bedroom, gesturing for Pete to take a look. Pete pushed open the door. Ray was curled up on the cot wrapped in a blanket. There was a pile of blood-soaked cloths and blankets on the floor. The air was thick and cloying. It caught in his throat. He grabbed the pile of wretched cloths and dumped them outside. Dwain stood silently behind Ma, his rough hand resting gently on her shoulder.

'Ma, what happened Ma? said Pete, his voice quiet and strained. 'Did Ray have the baby?'

Sally didn't reply, her eyes cast down at the table. Pete glanced at Dwain, asking again, with more strength in his voice.

'Ma, you got to tell me what's happened. Is Ray OK? And what about the baby?'

Sally raised her head and stared at Pete, exhaustion in her face, lines deep and shadowed, eyes sunken and red.

'Pete... Oh Pete. It's all over, son.'

'Ma, you're not making sense, you got to tell me what's happened. Where's the baby Ma?'

When she replied Sally's voice was drenched with pain.

'The baby's gone Pete. It had to go, it really did. She couldn't keep that baby it would be wrong. This way it's for the best for everyone.'

Before Pete could respond Dwain spoke up. Eyes avoiding Pete, his voice flat, he echoed Sally's words,

'It's best for everyone Pete, the baby didn't live.'

Pete took in a deep breath. He didn't understand what was going on. Why would it be better that the baby died? He could feel a mix of emotions surging to the surface. He didn't understand how he felt. Was it grief? Was it anger? He looked at Ma slumped in front of him and he felt his anger rising.

How could she let the baby die? His baby.

He tried to stay calm.

'Ma, tell me what happened? Where's my baby?'

Sally shook her head, devoid of words. Dwain spoke for her.

'Pete, take a step back. Ma needs some time. Can't you see she's exhausted. Seems the baby died while Ray was birthing it. You won't appreciate it now, but it's the best thing for everyone.'

'Why?' Pete screamed. 'Why is it best for everyone? What about me! How is this best for me?'

Tears were streaming down Sally's face; she turned away from Pete. Dwain stood between them. When he spoke there was a tremble in his voice.

'Ray's your sister Pete,' he said, 'she's Ma's daughter.'

Pete grabbed the table to stop himself falling.

'How?'

That simple word was barely audible. Dwain squeezed Pete's shoulder, as if to share his strength.

'It was a long time ago Pete, you was so small. Some men came by when Pa was in town. You was asleep, but I woke up. I saw it happen from the door. They raped our Ma. When it was over I sat in the dirt with Ma, till Pa got back. I didn't know at the time, what had happened, not really, I was too young. But Ma got bigger and bigger and Pa got so mad. You remember that, don't you, Pete?'

Pete nodded. Yes, he remembered his Pa so angry and frightening.

'Anyways, when it was time for the baby to come, Pa got Lena Crow out here to see to Ma, and he took you and me into town. When we got back, Ma was sick but she got better and there was no baby. Pa calmed down a bit after that, he just took to spending more time drinking and gambling in town.'

Pete stood there swaying in silent confusion. Dwain held on to him, waiting for a spark of understanding.

'Pete, I remember when I was around fourteen year old, I was in town with Pa and we saw the Crow family. Melvin and Lena had Ray with them, she was just a kid then. She was a strange looking girl with her red hair and pale skin, and those eyes like nothing I'd ever seen before. They was the palest blue. And she looked nothing like Melvin or Lena. I think Pa just knew when he looked at her, that she was Ma's child. He told Melvin Crow that he wasn't to bring the girl into town ever again. That she was an abomination and should have been dead. I didn't understand it at the time.'

Dwain breathed deep staring into his brother's eyes.

'Thing is, the man that raped Ma looked just like Ray. I saw him Pete, and I'll never forget what he looked like. She looks just like him. Pa knew the baby hadn't died. That Lena Crow had taken it. He got mad again after that. He'd beat up on Ma, and us. It was like he remembered everything all over again and it just made him mad. That's when I figured it out. That's why I didn't want you around her. I just couldn't tell you.'

Dwain's words hit Pete like lead bullets, they sunk deep, 'cos Pete knew them to be true. He looked up at Dwain, but he offered no more words. He shrugged off his brother's strong hand and walked out the door. He swung himself into the saddle and turned away from the cabin. Spurring his horse to a gallop, he slackened the reins letting it find its own direction. Dwain stood on the veranda watching him go, tears misting his eyes.

Thirty-five

Sheriff Boone found Pete sitting in the saloon with a large mug of coffee on the table in front of him. According to Bob Wallace, Pete had turned up the night before. He hadn't said much, just set about drinking whiskey until he plumb fell down on the floor.

They'd put him in an upstairs room for the night and as dawn broke he'd found his way downstairs again. Sheriff Boone took in the grey tinge of his skin and his sunken bloodshot eyes. He sure looked like a man who'd drunk a skinful, but there was something else. He looked haunted. The Sheriff knew men like Pete Mickleton don't drink themselves unconscious without reason. He pulled up a chair and sat opposite Pete, waiting silently for him to say something.

Eventually, after several gulps of coffee, Pete raised his eyes to the Sheriff. When he spoke his voice was thick with last night's whiskey and a night of bad dreams.

'What d'you want Sheriff? Ain't in no mood for casual conversation.'

The Sheriff noted the tremor in Pete's hands as he raised the coffee to his lips.

'Well, son, I hear you hit the whiskey hard last night. Thought it was my duty to check on you. There some problem out your place has you hiding in a bottle?'

Pete's mouth formed into a hard line. Slowly, deliberately, he lowered his coffee to the table. Crossing his arms he leaned back, like he was increasing distance between them.

'Sheriff, it ain't your problem what goes on at my place. You don't need to be poking your nose into Mickleton business.'

'Well son, seeing as how I still have a property dispute, and two murders unaccounted for, I'm thinking what goes on at your place might just be my business. Besides, I've been meaning to have a talk with you. Doc tells me Ray's account of the night of the murders ain't exactly what you told me.'

The Sheriff paused. Bo entered the saloon, heading in their direction. He met the Sheriff's eye, nodded to Pete and walked past them to the bar. The Sheriff's attention returned to Pete, sitting silent and rigid in his chair.

'Thing is, Pete', the Sheriff continued, 'the only suspects I got for the murders of Cole and Audley is you and Ray. Now I been thinking this whole time, that it was most likely you went out there and shot them dead for what they did to Ray. Maybe she told you to, maybe she asked you to, or maybe you just took it on yourself to dish out some rough justice. But just lately I got me thinking a bit harder. Why would Ray Crow tell the Doc you wasn't with her that night? Why would she say you was with Dwain, when I know you wasn't. Ain't just Dwain and your Ma telling me he was at the ranch that night, I got ranch hands saying he was there. Then I got them same people, and you, telling me you weren't. So, why is Ray trying to implicate you and Dwain? Can you answer me that, son?'

Pete remained silent.

'No, son, I didn't think so. You see, I'm coming round to the conclusion that Ray weren't quite hurt so bad as we all thought she was. I'm reckoning she went and dealt some justice to them boys that hurt her. I always figured she didn't have it in her to kill in cold blood. But hurt and pain can do a lot of things, and just maybe it done enough to make that girl into a killer. And now here you are, in a world of hurt. You need to talk to me, son. You need to start telling me the truth.'

Pete knew the Sheriff was right, he'd come to the same conclusion. His world was unravelling. He'd lied to protect Ray, and their baby. He thought once the baby came they would find a way to be together, to live as a family. The deaths of those drifters would be forgotten. That between them, him and Ray would forge something new. The baby would be a way of writing the future the way it should be, rubbing out past mistakes. But now there was no baby. And not only that, Ray was his half-sister. He felt shame burning in the pit of his stomach. Jesus, he wanted to throw up.

The Sheriff noted the turmoil on Pete's face. He reached his hand slowly to his holster. He wasn't sure which way this would go. He spoke gently, his words softly crossing the space between them.

'Pete son, tell me what happened, that night?'

'I don't know, Sheriff,' said Pete, words catching in his throat.

All I know is, I got over to Ray's place and there weren't no-one there. I heard the gunshots just as I got there. Two of them, one after the other. Then I went inside, lit a fire, and heated me some food.'

The Sheriff leaned forward, his words insistent.

'When did Ray arrive, Pete?'

'Just a while after I heard the gun shots. Don't rightly know how long after.'

The Sheriff leaned back in his seat, exhaling tension from his body. He looked at Pete carefully. The boy looked broken. He stood and placed a hand on Pete's shoulder.

'Son, you need to come with us. We're riding out to your place.'

Pete looked up his eyes wet with tears.

'She had the baby, Sheriff, but it didn't live.'

The Sheriff squeezed Pete's shoulder. He nodded to Bo.

'We're riding now.'

The Sheriff road hard to the Mickleton Ranch. Pete was beside him with Bo and Jim behind. The Doc brought up the rear in his buggy.

It was still early when the ranch came into view. Out front Sheriff Boone reined his horse. Pete and the deputies drew up behind him. Dwain called out from the veranda, Sally standing close behind.

'What brings you out here so early, Sheriff, and is that my brother behind you?'

Dwain fixed his eyes on Pete, slumped in his saddle. He'd been worried about Pete since he'd ridden off the night before. By the looks of him, he'd gone into town and spent the night at the saloon, but that didn't explain why he'd been escorted home by the Sheriff and the deputies.

The Sheriff remained mounted.

'Dwain,' he said, 'we've come out to see Ray. I've reason to believe that she's responsible for the murders of Cole and Audley.'

He nodded across to Pete.

'Now Pete here tells me that she's lost the baby, so I got the Doc on his way to check her out. He says she's fit and she'll need to be coming back into town with me.'

Sally stepped forward to stand next to Dwain. She clutched at her apron, her voice shaking.

'Sheriff, Ray just had the baby last night. She ain't well enough for this. It's not an easy thing for a woman, birthing. She needs to sleep and recover. Perhaps you can come back another day.'

She shook Dwain's arm. 'Dwain,' she implored, 'you have to do something.'

Dwain looked down at his Ma, pity in his eyes.

'Ma, I can't do nothing about this and you know it.'

Tears tumbled from Sally's eyes. There was a stabbing pain in her chest. This was her daughter they were talking about taking and arresting. And for what, killing men who'd attacked her?

'Sheriff, she couldn't do it. She couldn't have killed those men. Pete told you that he was with her.'

Sally looked over at Pete. He sat silent on his horse. His gaze blank. He couldn't, or wouldn't meet her eye. Sally felt herself slipping, the earth moving away from her. She needed to protect her daughter. The daughter she both loved and feared. The daughter that she didn't understand. Her child. She felt herself let out a primal, animal sound.

Dwain grabbed her to stop her falling.

Thirty-six

Ray balanced on the edge of a precipice. The earth almost invisible below. Endless sky stretching out in front of her. The atmosphere was clear, but storm clouds loomed on the horizon. Ray felt their pull. She yearned to step off the edge, to be lifted on the updraft. Her wings twitched, yearning to unfold. She felt hollowed out inside, but on the outside she felt jagged and coarse. There was an overwhelming urge to allow herself to be drawn up into the coming storm. To be tossed and turned like a pebble in a stream, polished by the elements until she was smooth and devoid of feeling.

She looked for Earl. But he wasn't to be seen; she felt his absence keenly. She waited for him to arrive as he always had. Seconds turned into minutes. She couldn't wait any longer. The desire for oblivion was too strong. But just as she was about to step off, she was pulled back from the edge. She opened her eyes to sun pouring into the room and Earl's face above her.

'Come back, come back,' he was calling. 'Come back, they need you Ray.'

Bit by bit, feeling came back to her body. She felt like when she'd taken that beating, bruised and weak. But this time she ached between her legs something awful. She stared down at her belly, still rounded but shrunk, empty — bereft of life. She glanced up at Earl, seeking explanation, meaning.

'They need you Ray,' he whispered, his hand stroked her forehead filling her with strength.

Ray dragged herself out of bed. She found a fresh shirt and pants. Grabbing her hat she buckled on her holster. She felt strengthened by Earl's presence. Her back was twitching where her wings should be; she felt them yearning to unfold. Tottering to the main door she peeked out of a crack. There was the Sheriff on his big mare. Behind him were his shadows, Jim and Bo, and behind them was Pete. She thought back to the night she'd seen the Sheriff and his deputies standing outside her cabin. That night they came to tell Ma that Pa had died. It seemed so long ago. She was a different person then.

Pete looked broken. She wondered what the Sheriff wanted with him. Earl was at her shoulder; she could feel his strength bleeding into her. Together, they walked outside onto the veranda. She felt her wings jerk with the need to unfold, to spread, to be free, but she held them back. She could feel anger rising, fermenting with confusion and loss.

All she wanted was love and some peace to enjoy it. She yearned for a place to call home, where she could drift with the pattern of the seasons, to be part of the earth and the sky. She craved the musky smell of Rio, his friendship and comfort, and then remembered that he'd gone — poisoned and burned. She stared at the men out front and saw their faces darken, becoming cruel masks. In her mind, every one of them sought to control her and tether her to the ground. Even if they showed kindness now, cruelty would surely emerge.

The Sheriff's strident voice cut through her thoughts.

'Ray Crow, we need to talk to you about the murders of Audley and Cole. I have reason to believe that you killed those men. I understand you probably don't feel quite yourself at the moment. I got the Doc coming along shortly and I'd like him to take a look at you, before we take this any further.'

Ray was silent, absorbing the Sheriff's words. Audley and Cole deserved to die, and she felt no remorse for her actions. She knew the consequences, but she wasn't going to accept them. Why was it that men could attack her, beat her, and try and wrest her home from her, but she couldn't fight back. She couldn't exact justice for herself. She raised her eyes upwards to the heavens. She needed to fly. She couldn't live tethered to the ground, trapped on the earth in this world, not as it is now. She felt Earl next to her, his hand comforting on her shoulder. She raised her arms slowly from her sides. She heard the Sheriff again, there was urgency in his voice.

'What are you doing Ray? We just want to talk for the moment, but we are armed, and we will uphold the law.'

The Sheriff sat upright in his saddle scrutinising Ray's every move. Slowly he lowered his hand to his pistol. He had a bad feeling about this, and he'd long since learned to listen to his gut. The air felt electric; storm clouds were forming overhead; the sky was beginning to darken. He watched Ray staring up to the heavens, her arms held out by her sides. She was smiling, but there was a fierce tension in her body. Her shadow seemed to be growing, spilling out of the veranda, covering the ground like a giant cloak.

He kept his eyes focussed on the gun in her holster. He could sense Bo and Jim behind him. He knew Jim would be squaring up his rifle and Bo's hand would be ready to rip his gun from his holster. On the veranda, Dwain was feeling the tension too. Deep in her shadow, he'd moved away from Ray as far as he could. At the other end of the veranda he shielded Sally behind him. His gaze darted nervously between Ray and the men on the horses, hand on his gun, ready to act. The Sheriff spoke again, his voice slow and steady, entreating for calm.

'Ray, I'm going to need you to unbuckle your belt and drop your holster. Slow now, I need to see that holster on the ground.'

Ray slowly lowered her head to look out at the men in front of her. The Sheriff was sitting rigid on his horse, his face taut, his gaze unflinching. Behind the Sheriff, Jim had a rifle aimed at her. Bo had his attention on Pete, who still sat slumped in his saddle, as if unaware of what was going on.

Ray could feel Earl's hand resting on her shoulder, keeping her feet planted on the ground. Her wings burned with the desire to be free. She couldn't help it, there was too much emotion to hold in. All the pain, anger and loss gushed up to the surface. She could contain it no more. Her wings convulsed and sprang from her back. Their vast span darkening the sky. Pete lifted his head; their eyes met. In that moment she knew him for what he was, broken and flawed, just like her. She would take him with her, keep him safe. She smiled at him and felt her wings beat, ready to transport her into the sky.

Pete returned Ray's gaze. He recognised her pain, but there was also hope in her eyes. It may be he's lost the baby, but he wasn't going to lose Ray. Regardless of everything, he loved her; he would stand for her, he would protect her. He would do what he should have done a long time ago — put her first. The sky became ever darker, the air swirled around him.

Pete tugged his reins, wheeling his horse away from the Sheriff and deputies. His hand reached for his pistol, eyes on Ray.

As the wind gusted about the Sheriff a giant shadow blotted out the sun. His horse reared in confusion and fear. He heard Pete's horse charge up behind him. An instant later Pete blazed past, low in the saddle, gun in his hand, riding towards Ray.

Dwain grabbed Sally, urging her to safety, drawing his gun. The deputies spurred their horses to intercept Pete.

The Sheriff's pistol hung slack in his hand. He stared at Ray open mouthed. As she grew in size, darkness was spreading around her. Fear clutched at his belly; hands shaking, he raised his gun. Great gusts of wind buffeting him, flying dust blurred his vision. His mount tossed her head, snorting and stamping the ground. He felt her fear; she'd soon turn and stampede out of there. In the darkness and confusion, he registered men shouting, the pounding of hooves and gunshots.

From within the eye of this storm he couldn't tell who had fired or at what. The great shadow became bigger and darker. Within its boundaries all was wind, dust, confusion and fear. All he could see clearly was Ray. She was rising up into the darkness. He pulled the trigger. His aim wasn't Ray; he'd fired to kill his fear. His horse whirled on the spot. Through tearing eyes he saw Pete fall, his chest ripped open spraying red against the blackness of the sky. The Sheriff's horse wheeled round and around; he fought to stay seated. The wind was deafening. A riderless horse tore past him, the air was ripped from his lungs.

A huge vortex of swirling dust dragged him from his horse. The darkness was complete, sand scoured his face, he staggered to his feet feeling his way forward arms outstretched like a blind man. Dust clogged his throat, he lost his footing, flying, upwards, sideways, arms flailing, out of control. He opened his mouth to breathe, but there was no air. No air to feed his dust filled lungs. His vision narrowed; he felt his heart explode. Pain shot through him — time stopped.

Everything became clear.

Ray was above him, riding the wind. Her pale blue eyes glistening and her flaming hair burning bright. Her giant black wings beat fiercely. She looked at him, he at her. Her wings flexed, sharp talons scooped him up, darkness descended, and his pain disappeared.

Thirty-seven

The Doc shuddered; the air was rapidly cooling around him. He looked up at the darkening sky. With a shiver he snapped the reins; his horse broke into a trot. The buggy jolted along the unmade track raising an impenetrable cloud of ochre dust. The wind increased and a spiralling dust devil overtook him. He tugged a handkerchief from his pocket, pressing it against his face, squinting against the whirling dirt. Foreboding gnawed at the pit of his belly. The sky darkened; peels of thunder reverberated across the landscape. Something was very wrong at the Mickleton place.

A gunshot rang out; he reined his horse to a grinding halt. He braced himself against the blinding onslaught of dust, eyes darting left and right, unsure of what his next move should be. More gunshots, too many to count. He ducked to the floor of the buggy, heart racing.

After a while, the firing stopped leaving a leaden silence. The wind calmed, the dust began settling; he glimpsed the sky, dark and grey. Despite his deep foreboding, He clucked to his horse and flicked the reins. His every instinct was to turn his rig round and high tail it to the safety of town. Reluctantly he continued heading for the ranch. It wasn't long before he was passing through the arched gateway, and the ranch buildings were coming into view.

Open mouthed he took in the scene of carnage. Bo and Jim were lying crumped in the dirt, bullet wounds gaping, blood staining the thirsty ground. In front of the veranda was Dwain, cradling Pete's blood-soaked body. Sally sprawled on the ground beside them, her streaming eyes devoid of comprehension. The Doc grabbed his bag and ran to them.

Dwain looked up, struggling for words. When they came they tore at his throat

'Too late Doc. Nothing you can do for him.'

The Doc eyeballed Dwain and Sally; neither appeared injured. He tore open Pete's blood-saturated shirt exposing a gaping wound in his chest, his pulse was failing fast. Dwain was correct; it was too late for Pete.

Where's the Sheriff in all this? The Doc located him lying by the body of his horse, his eyes wide staring up into the sky. No pulse: the Sheriff too was beyond help.

Like it was the most natural thing, the Doc saw to the health of the Sheriff's horse. She was alive, stunned, shivers were twitching through her flanks. A few encouraging jerks on the reins and the Doc had her standing; he tutted.

At least someone benefited from his ministrations this day.

The Doc stood, dazed, looking around him. He felt awash with emotion: shock, outrage, sadness. But most of all he felt confusion. He didn't understand what had happened here. He made his way back over to Pete, once again kneeling on the ground, next to Dwain and Sally. He placed a hand on Dwain's arm and spoke gently.

'What happened here, Dwain, and where's Ray, is she inside?'

Dwain's response was flat, emotionless.

'Gone, Doc.'

The Doc looked around. Ray's body was nowhere in sight; had she ridden off?

'What do you mean, she's gone, Dwain, gone where?'

'Can't explain, Doc. Can't explain nothing. She's just gone. Don't know any other way of sayin' it. And she ain't coming back.'

The Doc sat back on his heels. He tried Pete's pulse, it barely registered. He minutes, seconds maybe. Pete's face, his eyes were closed, expression serene. Wherever he was, pain wasn't touching him.

Pete rested on the dirt. Above it for now, but he knew he hadn't long before it swallowed him. Ray was hovering above him. Her eyes portals to a clear summer sky. Hair teased by the wind the colours of a sunset. She looked happier than he could remember. Her spreading wings pulsing gently. Amongst the glistening black feathers iridescent purples and greens, spun with flecks of gold. Pete felt happy; this was all he'd ever yearned for.

A thought penetrated his bliss.

The baby!
'It's OK,' said Ray, 'she's fine.'
She brushed her hand across his forehead; anxiety evaporated. There was just the heat of the sun, the power of the wind, and the weight of the earth. Ray's arms enfolded him, raising him from the ground. He felt her warmth, and the slow beat of her powerful wings. Peace and contentment cocooned him. There was only this moment — and he needed nothing else.

Dwain stood taking in the carnage around him. His heart felt heavy and for the first time in his life he felt tears flowing freely. He looked down at his brother's lifeless body, still and surprisingly peaceful in spite of the ragged, gaping wound in his chest. His mother's bent body slumped over that of his brother, shaking as she cried. He watched the Doc walk toward him shaking his head.

'They're all dead, Dwain,' he said sadly. He raised a questioning eyebrow.

'I only fired in self-defence, Doc,' Dwain shook his head, like a man waking from a living nightmare. 'I don't remember much. Like it wasn't real, nothing made sense. I can't tell you if I shot anyone. But if I did, then I'm telling you, Doc, it was self-defence.'

Self-defence from what?

The Doc squeezed Dwain's shoulder.

'It's all over now, boy. There ain't anything me, or anyone else can do to bring these boys back.'

The Doc looked around.

'And Ray is nowhere to be seen, so I guess we can assume she played a part in this. The Marshall will need to know. We'll get a new Sheriff, and by then Ray Crow will no doubt be long gone. Guess, you can tell this story any which way you like, Dwain. You're the only one left can tell it.'

They stood in silence listening to the muffled weeping of Sally and feeling the now gentle breeze in the air. The sky began to darken again slightly and both men looked anxiously upwards. Grey clouds were forming above them. Dwain turned back to the Doc.

'I guess, we should get these boys into your rig so you can get them back to town. It ain't fitting to leave them here in the dirt.' The Doc nodded.

'What about Pete? Should I take him into town, too?'

'Pete stays,' said Dwain, 'this is his home; I'll bury him here.'

The Doc nodded. They approached the nearest body, their footsteps heavy, weighted with sadness. Between them they loaded the bodies into Doc's buggy, covering them with blankets as the flies began to land. Dwain hitched the loose horses to the back before the Doc took his seat. He looked down at Dwain for a long moment, his mind in turmoil.

'Dwain, I'll be seeing you around, no doubt. I'll be telling the Marshall just what I heard and saw. Hell, think I saw, I'll tell him this ain't none of your doing. Rest assured on that.'

Dwain watched the over-laden buggy roll ponderously through the distant gates. He headed back to where Sally was stooped over Pete's body. He gripped her shoulder in a silent benediction. After a while, he walked to the barn to fetch a shovel, picturing himself pecking at the hard baked soil. He'd dig until the dullness of the earth near broke his back, knowing along with his brother, he'd be burying a piece of himself. The stabbing ragged pain he felt would fade, but the numbness, he knew, would be a lifelong companion. He'd run the ranch and care for his Ma. But without Pete nothing could be the same.

As Dwain neared the barn a large raven landed on the roof ridge. He felt its bright intelligent eyes follow him as he walked across the yard. It hopped impatiently from one foot to the other above him, its beak opening and closing calling softly. *Caaaw, caaaw*. The closer he got, the more agitated the bird became, nodding its head *caaawing* louder. Dwain avoided its eyes, and was relieved to duck into the barn. The air was cooler in the barn. Dwain was startled by the call of another raven perched on the rail separating the horses' stalls. This one sat still with its head tilted to one side as it watched him. The horses didn't seem to be bothered by its presence. As he watched, the bird dropped down from the rail and began to peck at a rumpled blanket on a pile of straw. It raised its eyes to Dwain and then hopped back up onto the rail.

Dwain looked from the bird to the pile on the ground and after a moment's hesitation took tentative steps forward. The bird stayed put like a faithful guardian angel. Dwain peeled back the blanket. And there was the vulnerable body of a baby girl. His breath caught in his throat; his heart hammered in his chest; he dropped to his knees. He gently brushed her cheek with the back of his calloused hand. She blinked and smiled, a tiny hand reaching up to him. He choked on his breath. It was alive. Pete's baby was alive. Dwain gently pulled the blankets around her; cradling her against his chest.

Dwain stood, looking down at the baby. Her eyelids flickered and then opened wide. He looked down into deep brown eyes and in that moment, he saw his brother. With a deep breath, he walked out of the barn into the sunlight.

His attention was drawn to two birds flying high, silhouetted by the sun. He watched them until they disappeared from view, at that moment, he felt first one, then another drop of rain.

He stood still, his face raised to the heavens, his eyes closed as the breeze blew and the rain began to fall. Large, clean, cool droplets of natural water, pure enough to wash the earth clean.

THE END

Acknowledgements

To the wonderful ladies of book club – your insights and encouragement have been invaluable. Susan, your unwavering support means the world to me. J.B., writer and gentleman, thanks for getting me to the line, and Paul, thanks for getting me over it — I couldn't have done it without you. Mum, I will forever appreciate the gift of wanting to write. Madeleine, your honesty and support means the world to me. And to Steve, my person - there are simply not enough words to express my love and gratitude.

Dear Reader

I would love to get your feedback.

If you liked Crow Girl, may I ask you to post a quick review.

Your reviews make a massive difference to independent authors, like me, who don't have the weight of a traditional publishing house behind them.

Thank you!

What other readers are saying about Crow Girl:

'Crow Girl – an exceptional read'

'Gem of a book'

'Great read!!'

Printed in Great Britain
by Amazon